Lone Star Ranger:

Volume 4

A Ranger's Christmas

James J. Griffin

Lone Star Ranger:
Volume 1 A Ranger to Ride With
Volume 2 A Ranger to Reckon With
Volume 3 A Ranger to Fight With

Lone Star Ranger Vol.4:
A Ranger's Christmas by James J. Griffin
Copyright© 2014 James J. Griffin
Cover Design Livia Reasoner
Texas Ranger badge image courtesy of the Texas Ranger
Hall of Fame and Museum, Waco
Author photo credited to Susanne Onatah
Painted Pony Books
www.paintedponybooks.com

Dedication

For Everyone Who Has Ever Had to Spend Their Holidays Away From Home, Family, and Loved Ones.

Prologue

Nate Stewart crawled gratefully under his blankets. It was the evening of the day after the Rangers' gunfight with the outlaws who had killed Nate's parents and older brother, along with so many others. Nate, like the rest of the men, was still feeling drained after the hard chase, followed by the tension and, yes, Nate had to admit it, raw fear of the final showdown with the renegades. In addition, the wounded found it difficult to maintain a hard pace, so Captain Quincy had kept his Rangers' horses moving mostly at a walk. That meant they had not covered the distance they ordinarily would. They made camp early, well before sundown, cared for the mounts, then ate a quick supper. Before dusk had even faded to full dark, most of the men were asleep. Now, except for the two sentries, it seemed to Nate he was the only one still awake. He'd spent some extra time grooming his sorrel, Big Red, before turning in.

Nate lay on his back, his hands behind his neck, his head pillowed on his saddle. Lost in thought, he gazed up at the myriad stars pin-pricking the inky curtain of the night sky. A thin crescent moon was just lifting itself over the eastern horizon. He reflected on all that had happened to him since the attack on his family's ranch, the murder of his parents and older brother, and himself being shot and left for dead. Although it had only been a few weeks since that fateful day, sometimes Nate's recollection seemed hazy, as if the event had happened many months ago. Other times, his memories were as vivid as if the outlaws had attacked only yesterday.

Nate sighed. After the final confrontation between the Rangers and the gang, during which he had finally shot and killed the pale-eyed demon leading the outfit, he had expected to feel triumphant, or at least a deep satisfaction at finally exacting his revenge on the murderers. Instead, he just felt weary. There seemed to be a hollowness deep in his soul. True, he was appreciative that the men were dead, and would never again rob, burn, and kill. He was glad of that. And his parents' and brother's deaths had been avenged. But the deaths of the outlaws would not bring back his family, nor Nate's old life. Justice had been served, but at what cost?

Nate shifted slightly. One thing was for certain. He was no longer the clumsy, naïve youngster he'd been before all this happened. Unlike Jonathan, his older brother, who had instinctively taken to Texas and the cowboy life, Nate had hated his new home, and desired nothing more than to return to Wilmington, Delaware, and his old friends. He'd been like a fish out of water, feeling incompetent, lost, and completely out of place. Now, after being rescued by the Rangers, and becoming part of the outfit, he'd discovered a new life, one he loved. Under their careful tutelage, the Rangers had taught Nate how to handle himself on the rugged western frontier, not only to survive, but to thrive. He only wished his ma and pa, and especially his older brother Jonathan, could see him now. He realized he still had some more growing up to do, and a lot to learn, but he was certain he could handle almost anything which Texas, and the outlaws who roamed its vast spaces, could throw at him. And he knew one thing for sure. Whatever happened from here on out, his old life was behind him, and the new one certainly promised to be filled with adventure.

1

Two days after leaving the Devil's River, about mid-afternoon, Captain Quincy ordered the column of men to a halt. He pointed at a fast-growing smudge of dust on the northern horizon.

"What do you make of that dust off to the northwest, Bob?" he asked Lieutenant Berkeley. "Seems like there's an awful lot of it. I reckon it's a dust storm comin' up on us, and it looks like it's movin' right quick. If it is, we'd better find somewhere to hole up, and fast. We sure don't want to be caught out in the open when that storm hits."

Bob pushed back his Stetson, then pulled it off and rubbed sweat from the inside band. He shoved it back on his head, then studied the dust cloud before replying.

"I dunno, Dave. I doubt it's a dust storm. I know the wind can blow up one heckuva storm with no warnin', but the weather doesn't seem right for one to me. There's hardly any breeze at all, yet that cloud's movin' mighty fast. That dust's also not spread out far enough. It seems to be comin' from one spot. I'd say whatever is causin' it is man-made. But it sure ain't Indians. No Comanche, Apache, or Kiowa worth his salt would stir up that much of a dust cloud."

"Jeb, ride on back and bring up Percy, will you?" Quincy asked Ranger Rollins.

"Right away, Cap'n Dave," Jeb answered. He started to turn Dudley, his paint, back along the column, but stopped when Percy Leaping Buck, the Rangers' Tonkawa scout, rode up.

"There's no need to send Jeb lookin' for me," Percy said, as he pulled Wind Runner, his wiry pinto gelding, to a stop. "I'm right here. Knew you'd want me."

"You always have had fine instincts, Percy," Quincy said. "That's why you're such a valuable member of this outfit. Now, what do you make of that dust cloud yonder? Think you should scout ahead and see what's causin' it?"

"There's no need for that," Percy answered. "I'm surprised none of you boys haven't already figured it out. That dust is from a herd of buffalo, a big one, stampeding straight at us. From the way they're movin', it won't be long until they're right on top of us. Which means, if we don't get out of their way, we'll be trampled flatter'n George's hotcakes."

"There sure ain't no place to hide from 'em around here," Jeb said. "We'll have to try'n outrun those buffs."

"Jeb, you know a man on horseback can't outrun a stampeding herd of buffalo," Percy said. "A lotta horses might be able to run a bit faster than buffalo, but they sure can't outlast 'em. A frightened buffalo'll run all day if he has to, or jump straight over a cliff and kill himself. Any horse in front of that stampede would wear himself out and get plumb run down, while those buffs wouldn't even be breathin' hard. No, I figure our only chance is that low mesa over there, off to the left. We'd best hope we can find some kind of trail to the top, or perhaps a cut in its side we can all squeeze into. If there aren't any, then we'll have to try to beat that herd to the far end of that mesa, huddle up against the wall, and hope those buffalo go on past us. And with some real luck, I might even be able to down one or two of 'em, so we'll have fresh meat. But we've got to get movin', and I mean right now. That herd'll be here before we know it. It's gonna be a real close call beating it to the mesa. We keep sittin' here jawin', and we won't stand a chance. Especially George and the chuck wagon."

"Then let's get movin'," Captain Quincy said. He turned his bay, Bailey, to face the rest of the men.

"Boys," he shouted, "That dust cloud's from a stampedin' herd of buffalo. We've got to try and outrun 'em to the back side of that mesa up ahead. So run your horses like the devil himself was after you, because if you don't, some of you just might be meetin' up with him, or mebbe the Good Lord's angels, today. Good luck."

He reined Bailey around and dug his spurs into the horse's ribs. Bailey leapt forward into a dead run, the rest of the men strung out behind him, with George in the chuck wagon, then Phil and the remuda, bringing up the rear. The horses, used to running at top speed over the roughest terrain, needed little urging to maintain the breakneck pace.

"We gonna be able to outrun that stampede?" Nate called to Hoot, shouting to be heard over the horses' thundering hooves and labored breathing.

"You'd darn well better hope so," Hoot hollered back. "I've seen men killed in cattle stampedes, more'n once. It's not a pretty sight, and I'd imagine gettin' trampled by a herd of buffalo would be even worse. I sure don't want to die that way. I'd sooner take a bullet, any day. So just lay over your horse's neck and give him his head. Let him run until he's run out. You just might save your neck if you do."

Stung by the fear and urgency in Hoot's voice, Nate bent as low as he could over Big Red's withers, and slapped the reins against his neck, getting still more speed out of the long-legged sorrel. Within moments, Red was even overtaking Jeb's speedy paint, Dudley. Jeb's gelding had long been the fastest mount in Captain Quincy's company, but right now, Red was pushing him for all he was worth.

Occasionally, one of the men would turn in his saddle and risk a glance backward. The dust cloud from the stampeding buffalo was growing nearer every minute.

"They're gainin' on us fast," Joe Duffy yelled. "It's gonna be awful close." He pushed his horse even harder. Behind him, George was cursing and yelling at his mules, slapping the reins on their rumps, struggling to keep them under control. His wagon was jouncing wildly, every bump jolting its wheels off the ground, every chuckhole threatening to rip off an axle, every rut sending it swerving, nearly out of control. More than once it rose onto two wheels and nearly tipped over, only George's skill as a driver and a lot of luck bringing it back down on all four.

In what seemed like hours, but what was in reality less than ten minutes, the men reached the base of the mesa. They pulled their horses to a halt, while Percy took a quick look around.

"I don't see any way up this thing, and there's no clefts in the rocks we can find our way into," he said. "We've got to head for the far end, and huddle up against the base. That's our only chance. And hurry. Those buffs'll be right on top of us any minute now."

The menacing dust cloud had grown ominously close, and the buffalo herd had drawn near enough the pounding of their hooves could be heard. Just as the fatigued horses were pushed into a run once again, the buffalo thundered into view, still driven to frantic flight by whatever had panicked them. The Rangers' jaded mounts had no chance of outrunning the terror-stricken beasts for much longer. However, the sight, sound, and scent of those oncoming buffalo struck even more fear into the horses than their riders, so they needed no urging to use the last of their strength for a final, frantic burst of speed.

Nate was still close behind Jeb and Dudley when, without warning, Red stumbled and nearly went to his knees. Nate barely managed to stay in the saddle, gripping Red's sides desperately with his legs, to avoid being tossed over the falling horse's head. He pulled back on the reins as hard as he could, jerking Red's head up and keeping him from tumbling head over heels, and squashing Nate underneath his thousand pounds. The big sorrel resumed running, but at a much slower pace, and with a pronounced limp. Several of the other men had caught up to and passed Nate by the time he turned Red behind the shelter of the mesa's wall. The buffalo were hard on the heels of the last men to turn behind the wall.

Jake and Jill, the two mules pulling the chuck wagon, were completely panicked, so terrified George could hardly control them. When he attempted to turn them behind the mesa, they fought the reins, struggling to keep running straight ahead, then swerving so violently that the wagon overturned. George was thrown from his seat, landed hard on his face, slid for several feet, rolled over once, then lay still.

Phil Knight was just behind the wagon, driving the remuda and attempting to keep it bunched. When he saw George's fall, he left the spare animals to their own devices and spurred Parker, his chestnut, toward the unconscious cook. Dan Morton had also seen the wreck, and he also spurred Pedro, his buckskin, to where George had fallen. He and Phil reached George at the same time. They leapt from their saddles and hurried to him. When they started to drag him out of danger, they realized the buffalo herd was too close. They didn't have enough time to pull George to safety.

"Throw him over my horse, Dan, and I'll get him outta here," Phil shouted. "Quick!"

George was dead weight as the two men lifted him, then draped him over Parker's withers. As Phil jumped back into the saddle and galloped away, Dan turned to face the oncoming buffalo. He pulled his rifle from its boot, just before the frightened Pedro yanked the reins from Dan's grip and raced off. Dan knelt and emptied his rifle at the huge bull leading the stampede, and the cow alongside it. The two lead animals dropped, but the rest of the herd swerved around the carcasses and kept coming. Dan tossed aside the empty rifle, pulled out his pistol, and raced for the dubious shelter of the overturned wagon, emptying the gun as he ran. For a moment, it appeared he would reach safety, but one of the charging beasts hit him with its shoulder and knocked him off his feet. He disappeared under a thousand hooves as the herd raced on, some of them slamming into the wagon. The heavy conveyance shuddered under the impact, its canvas top ripping and sturdy wood planks splintering. The men who saw Dan go down grimaced, a couple of them whispering silent prayers, the rest cursing at his fate.

Phil galloped to safety and slid out of his saddle. "A couple of you give me a hand with George, here," he called. Hoot and Tom rushed to help him. They lifted the unconscious cook off Parker and laid him gently on the ground. Phil turned around to look for Dan.

"Where's Dan?" he cried, when he saw no sign of his partner.

"He didn't make it," Tom said, shaking his head. "His horse ran off. He tried to reach the chuck wagon, but he didn't make it. Those buffs trampled him into the dirt."

Phil hung his head, his shoulders shaking as he stifled a sob.

As Percy had hoped, the panicked buffalo continued running straight ahead, in their headlong dash. The men had to hold tight to their terrified horses' reins, until the stampede got by. It took several minutes for the last of the buffalo to pass. Once the herd had swept by, Captain Quincy ordered his men into action.

"Jim, see what you can do for George," he told Jim Kelly. "Joe, you and Carl try'n see for certain what happened to Dan. Maybe, just maybe, by some miracle, he survived that tramplin'."

"There probably won't be enough left of poor Dan to pick up with a spoon," Joe muttered. "I can't think of a worse way to die. Even gettin' gut-shot'd be a better way to go."

"I'm well aware of that," Quincy snapped. "But he deserves a decent burial, no matter what."

"We'll bring him back, Cap'n, whatever shape he's in," Carl said. "C'mon, Joe." He and Joe mounted their horses and headed for the overturned wagon.

"Phil, you'd better get after the remuda, before they're scattered from here to Mexico," Quincy continued. "Take Nate with you."

"Right, Cap'n," Phil said. "C'mon, Nate."

"I can't go with you, Phil," Nate answered. "Red's hurt. He almost fell back there, and now he's limpin'."

"Phil, I'll go with you," Jeb offered. "Nate, you stay here and give the rest of the boys a hand. You can't chance makin' your horse's injury worse, and mebbe even cripplin' him for life."

"Thanks, Jeb," Phil replied. To Nate he continued. "Try not to fret too much about Red. Soon as me'n Jeb have the spare animals rounded up, I'll check him over. I know you must be worried about him, but I'm certain he'll be fine."

"Nate," Jim said. "I could use a hand treatin' the injured men, if you wouldn't mind. George is the worst hurt, but a couple of the others got some scrapes and bruises. It'd be a good chance for you to learn a bit about doctorin', if you think you can handle it. Learnin' how to sew up a cut, or treat a broken bone or busted head, might just save your life, or one of your friend's, some day."

"Sure, Jim," Nate agreed. "I'll do my best."

"I knew you'd say yes, and I appreciate it," Jim said. "C'mon, let's get to work."

"Dakota, you and Tom butcher those buffalo Dan downed. Percy got one too, so get that one, also. Get as much meat off of 'em as you can. There's enough dry mesquite branches lyin' around to cook it all. What we can't eat tonight we'll take along. The rest of you, let's get over to what's left of the wagon, and see what supplies we can salvage," Captain Quincy said. "And here's hopin' the wagon's not busted up so bad we can't repair it."

"Better send a couple of men back to pick up the stuff some of the mules lost," Lieutenant Bob said. "Looks like three of 'em ditched their pack saddles durin' that run."

"You're right, Bob. You take Hoot and handle that chore."

"We'll try'n save everything we can," Bob said. "We'd better pray those buffalo didn't smash up all the goods. We've still got five days ahead of us before we reach Fort Stockton. That's a long way to go without any food or water."

"You heard him, boys," Quincy said. "Let's get to work."

****

"Nate, follow me," Jim ordered. He went over to where his palomino, Sundrop, was standing ground-hitched, took his canteen off the saddlehorn, and got the bag containing his medical supplies out of his saddlebag. Then he and Nate went to where George had been placed. The cook was still unconscious, the lower half of his left leg bent at an odd angle. His face was coated with blood. Most of the skin had been scraped raw when he was pitched onto the gravelly soil. Jim knelt alongside him.

"As you can see, Nate, George is still out cold," he said. "The first thing we've gotta do is try and bring him around. Open my kit and hand me one of the cloths from it, will you?"

"Sure," Nate answered. He did as requested, opening

the leather bag and rummaging around until he came up with a square piece of clean cloth. "This the one?"

"That's just fine," Jim said. "I'm gonna pour a bit of water over George's forehead. With luck, that will wake him up. I wish we had some cold water, but that can't be helped. His breathin's good and steady, so I don't think he's got any kind of severe brain injury, or a bad concussion. At least, I sure hope not. Then I'll hand you my canteen. Wet the cloth with some of the water. Not any more'n you have to, though. We'll need every drop we can spare if the water barrels got busted up when the wagon went over."

"Okay, Jim."

"Here goes." Jim poured a bit of water onto George's forehead and scalp, then handed his canteen to Nate. The water had the desired effect. George's eyelids flickered open, and he began to splutter.

"What the devil are you doin', Jim? Are you tryin' to drown me? Lemme up."

He tried to sit up, but Jim put a restraining hand on his shoulder.

"Just take it easy," he urged. "You took a bad spill when the wagon flipped. Don't try'n move until I see just how bad you're hurt."

"I gotta get to my mules," George insisted, struggling to rise. He screamed in agony when unbearable pain shot through his leg. He quit fighting Jim's grip.

"My leg. Feels...like it's...busted." George's voice was tight.

"That's what I've been tryin' to tell you, pard," Jim said. "I'm almost certain your leg *is* broke. And I don't know yet how bad you might be busted up inside. I don't want you movin' until I've had the chance to look you over. So stay still while I do just that. Nate's here to give me a hand."

"Nate? He's just a kid," George said.

15

"But he's a kid with a lot of guts," Jim answered. "You know that. Now shut up and let me get to work. I'm gonna clean up your face, first. It got scraped up pretty bad. Nate, hand me that cloth."

"Sure," Nate passed him the dampened rag. Jim used it to carefully wash blood and dirt from George's face.

"You've got some pebbles stuck under your skin. I'm gonna have to pull those out," Jim said. "First, I've got to pour some whiskey over your face to sterilize it. That's gonna sting like blazes."

"You think you could manage to trickle some of that red-eye into my mouth, long as you're at it?" George asked.

"I think that could be arranged," Jim answered, chuckling. "Just a bit, though. Most of my medicines and bandages were in your wagon. I'm not certain how much of them survived the spill, so I've got to conserve what I have. Nate, there's a small flask of whiskey in my bag. I'll need that, and the tweezers."

"Okay." Nate pulled out the requested items, and handed them to Jim, who uncorked the bottle and dribbled a meager amount over the scrapes on George's face. He allowed George a small sip, then dipped the tweezers into the whiskey.

"Keep as still as you can, George," he urged. "I know it won't be easy, but try. Nate, get behind him, and hold down his shoulders if you need to."

As soon as Nate was in position, Jim set to work, carefully removing several pebbles from under George's skin. Once finished, he poured some whiskey onto the cloth, and gently wiped that across George's face.

"There, that's done," he said. "Now, George, I'm just gonna poke and prod at you a bit, to see if you might have any broken ribs, or internal damage."

"Just get at it, will you?" George grumbled.

"All right." Jim pushed on George's sides, thumped his

chest. He pressed down on his belly, then punched it with the side of his fist, lightly.

"Any pain here? Here? How about here?"

"No," George answered, to each question.

"That's good news," Jim said. "At least it seems you don't have any internal injuries. There's no bleedin' from your mouth, nose, or ears, either, which is another good sign. Now, the easy part's over. I've got to start on your leg. It's most likely gonna have to be set. Nate, I'll want you to..."

Jim was interrupted by a shout from a short distance behind the chuck wagon. Carl was standing atop a small boulder, waving his arms over his head and yelling, frantically.

"Jim! Over here! We found Dan! He's still alive! Hurry up!"

"I'll be right there," Jim called back.

"Dan's alive?" Nate said. "That doesn't seem possible."

"What happened to Dan?" George asked.

"No time for that now. I'll explain later," Jim said. "Can you hang on a bit longer?"

"Yep. Reckon I don't have a choice, anyhow," George said. He managed a wan grin. "Go take care of Dan."

"Thanks, George. Nate, let's go."

Jim and Nate ran for Carl as fast as their legs would carry them. Carl had climbed down off the boulder, and was now with Joe. Both of them were hunkered alongside a very battered Dan Morton. His clothes were in shreds, his hat gone, every bit of exposed flesh a mass of cuts and bruises. Blood trickled from a deep cut, just over his bruised and swollen right temple. He was lying on his back, and looked up at Jim through eyes glassy with pain.

"Dan, I'm gonna patch you up. You'll be just fine," Jim said, with more confidence than he felt. "We thought for certain you were a goner. How'd you manage to avoid bein' trampled?"

"I don't rightly...know," Dan said, gasping. "Last thing I recollect...was...runnin' for my life. Then...buffalo...hit me. Don't...remember...a thing...after that."

"We found him in that little ditch, just behind the rock Carl was standin' on," Joe said. "It must've been just deep enough to protect him from that stampede. Appears as if the buffalo jumped over him, rather'n tramplin' him to ribbons. Still, he was all curled up in a ball, and not movin' at all, just like he was dead. It scared the livin' daylights outta me and Carl when we rolled him over and he let out a yell. We knew we shouldn't move him, but we had to get him into some shade."

"You both did just fine," Jim said. "Dan, by lookin' at you, I can tell you're in bad shape. But don't go thinkin' you're a goner. You ain't, not by a long shot. Now, I'm gonna start checkin' you, all over."

Jim knelt alongside Dan, and held up his right hand, with two fingers extended.

"How many fingers do you see, Dan?" he asked.

"Two," Dan answered.

"That's good. Your vision hasn't been affected, which means there probably isn't any brain injury. That cut on your head's mighty deep. It'll need some stitches. I want to see if you're hurt anywhere else, before I start in on that."

As he'd done with George, Jim poked and prodded Dan's body. When he pressed against Dan's left side, he howled with agony.

"That hurt just a bit, Dan?" Jim asked.

"Just a bit? You like to killed me, Jim, you..." Dan let loose with a string of curses.

"You ain't hurt all that bad, if you can cuss like that, pardner," Jim said. "However, as I suspected, you've got a couple of broken ribs. Now, I don't see any froth bubblin' from your mouth, and your breathin' ain't raspy, so I don't believe any of those ribs have punctured a lung...yet. But I've got to bind 'em up real tight to make sure they don't. That means I'll need some long strips of cloth. I can't use your shirt, since it's tore up so bad, so I reckon that means I'll have to use mine." He shrugged out of his shirt, revealing several old scars across his back. Despite himself, Nate gasped, involuntarily.

"Somethin' wrong, Nate?" Jim asked.

"No. Not really," Nate fibbed.

"Those scars on my back startle you?" Jim said. "Don't let 'em. I got those when I was a prisoner of the Yankees durin' the War, and they thought they could whip some information outta me. It didn't work. They found out us Texas boys don't break that easy. But, those days are gone, and best forgotten. Now, I need you to slice up my shirt."

He handed the garment to Nate. While Nate cut it into strips, Jim cut off what was left of Dan's shirt.

"Carl, Joe, I'll need you to sit Dan up, and hold him there until I'm finished," he ordered. "Nate, I'll need you to hand me the bandages when I ask, and to help keep them good and tight while I tie them around Dan."

Dan was helped to a sitting position. Carl and Joe supported him while Jim wrapped the bandages around his middle, pulled them tight, and knotted them in place.

"How's that feel?" he asked, once the last knot was tied.

"I can't hardly breathe," Dan answered.

"Good. That's how you're supposed to feel," Jim answered. "It's especially important you don't start coughin', but if you do, it's the bandages which will prevent worse damage. I'm plumb sorry those bandages have to be so tight, but it can't be helped, not unless you want to chance one of those busted ribs pokin' a hole through your lungs. Now, I'll need you to keep sittin' up while I stitch up that cut on your head. You're not feelin' faint, or dizzy, are you?"

"No, I'm not. Just kinda like I got the stuffin's kicked outta me," Dan said.

"Which you pretty much did," Jim replied. "It's also gonna hurt when I stitch that cut."

"I know that," Dan said. "I've been sewn up before. I'll get through it."

"Good," Jim said. "Now Nate, I want you to watch carefully while I fix this cut. Just about every man out here knows how to stitch up a wound, and you should, too. And don't be ashamed if you get kinda sick to your belly while you watch. That happens to most men the first time they work on a deep wound like this one."

"I'll be all right," Nate answered. "At least, I think so."

"That's the spirit, kid," Jim said. He gave Nate a reassuring grin. "Now, in my kit there's a heavy needle, along with some thick surgical thread. There's also a scalpel, which is kind of a long, sharp, skinny knife. Take those out and give them to me. Another cloth, too."

Nate found the needle and thread, as well as the scalpel and cloth. He gave them to Jim.

"Now, just like you should always do, you need to clean and sterilize whatever instruments you're using. Your hands, too. Sometimes that means heatin' a knife blade until it's good and hot, soakin' cloths in boilin' water, or dippin' them in alcohol or whiskey. Sometimes all of those things. You should also make certain the wound is as clean as possible."

Jim took the cloth, and doused it liberally with whiskey. He used it to wash dirt and dried blood out of the gash in Dan's scalp. He then poured more of the whiskey over the scalpel, as well as his hands.

"Nate, pay close attention, now," he ordered. "With a wound like this, you've got to cut away the ragged edges before you can suture it. Otherwise, you won't have good skin, which you need to hold the stitches. I'm also going to shave as much hair away from the wound as possible. You don't want hair left in any kind of wound, if you can help it. Dan, you ready?"

"As much as I'll ever be."

Jim took the scalpel, shaved the hair from around the cut, and sliced away the rough edges of the wound.

"It'll bleed some, of course, but that'll stop in a minute. Once it does, I'll take my stitches. While I'm waitin', I'll sterilize the needle and thread."

Jim dipped the needle and thread in the whiskey, then wiped away the fresh blood from Dan's scalp.

"Now watch close, Nate. You push the edges of the wound together, then take your stitches. Just like sewin' up your shirt or britches."

Efficiently, Jim sewed up the wound. He knotted off the thread after the last stitch, then cut away the excess.

"There, Dan. That wasn't too bad, was it?" he asked.

"No. It wasn't all that awful," Dan answered.

"I probably shouldn't say this," Nate said, "But remember when you were needlin' me and Andy after we landed in those cactus, and had to get the spines pulled out of our butts, Dan? Now I guess I can *needle* you."

"Those buffalo might not have killed me, but your jokes sure will, Nate," Dan said, with a groan.

"Enough of that," Jim said. "Dan, I've done all I can do for now. Nate and I have to get back to George. He's got a busted leg I've got to set. Carl, Joe, help Dan to where the rest of the men are. Don't put any more strain on his ribs than you have to. As I said, we don't want one of them shiftin' and puttin' a hole through a lung. I'd rather he was carried on a litter, but there's none handy. Dan, I'll check on you later, just to make certain there isn't somethin' I missed. Nate, let's go."

Dan was helped to his feet, and, with his arms draped around Carl and Joe's shoulders, headed for the mesa's base. Jim and Nate went back to where George still waited. When they reached him, he was still conscious, but sweat beaded his forehead. It was apparent he was in pain, and becoming feverish.

"How's Dan?" he asked. "And where's your shirt, Jim?"

"Dan's pretty busted up, but I think he'll be all right," Jim answered. "He's got some broken ribs, a deep cut on his head, which I had to stitch closed, and a whole mess of other hurts. I had to cut up my shirt for bandages to bind his ribs, to answer your other question. Now, it's time to set that leg. And I don't need to warn you, George, it's gonna be pure agony when I do. You've seen broken bones set before."

"Tell me somethin' I don't already know," George said. "Just gimme a minute to take my bandanna off, so I can shove it in my mouth and bite down on it."

"Of course."

George removed his bandanna from around his neck, rolled it up, and tied a knot in the middle. Biting down on the knot while Jim worked on his leg would alleviate at least some of the pain. It would also help George keep from screaming.

"George, I hate to do this, but I'm gonna have to cut open your pants leg to have a look at your leg," Jim said. "It's either that, or pull 'em off. And you won't be able to put 'em back on once that leg is splinted."

"Uh-uh. That ain't gonna happen." George shook his head. "The only one who takes my pants off, besides me, is my wife Rosita back in Austin. They stay right where they are, thank you very much."

"Then I'll have to rip them open. Nate, there's a pair of scissors in my bag," Jim said. "Get them for me, will you?"

"Sure, Jim." Nate opened the bag, removed the scissors, and handed them to Jim, who quickly cut open George's denims' left leg, along the seam. While George's leg was clearly broken, at least no bone protruded from the flesh.

"How bad is it?" George asked.

"Not quite as bad as I was afraid it was," Jim answered. "It's busted, but at least the bone didn't break through your skin. I'm gonna have to jerk the pieces back in place, then splint your leg until it's healed. You'll be laid up for quite a spell, and you might well end up with a permanent limp."

"But you won't have to saw off my leg? I couldn't stand that." George's voice shook with worry.

"No, I won't. It's nowhere near as bad as that," Jim assured him. "Now, I'll need somethin' to splint it. However, there's no wood around here. That's a problem."

"Jim, how about a piece off the chuck wagon?" Nate suggested. "There should be some I could pry off."

"No! You ain't bustin' up my wagon," George protested.

"George, I hate to point this out to you, but your wagon already *is* busted up," Jim said. "Nate, that's a good idea. I'd bet there's already some loose pieces I could use. They need to be straight, a little shorter than George's leg, and not too wide. Any of the planks will do. Also, grab a blanket from the rig. We'll need that to pad the leg, and some strips off it to hold the splint in place."

"I'll be back quick as I can," Nate promised.

****

When Nate reached the wagon, it had been pushed back upright, and was standing on its wheels. Jake and Jill had been untangled from their harness and removed from the traces. They were tied to the wagon's tail gate. Captain Quincy and the men helping him were picking up the scattered supplies, salvaging what they could, leaving the rest to the desert.

"Nate," Quincy said. "Carl and Joe told us Dan's gonna be all right, praise the Lord. How's George?"

"Jim thinks he'll be fine too, Cap'n, but he's got a broken leg," Nate answered. "He sent me for some wood to splint it. We figured a couple of pieces from the wagon will have to make do. Oh, and I need a blanket for paddin', too."

"Of course. Ken." Quincy called to Ken Demarest, who hurried over.

"Yeah, Cap'n Dave?"

"Nate needs two pieces of wood, so Jim can splint George's leg. Help him with that, will you? Also, get him a blanket from the wagon. Then, after you've done that, see if you can help Carl or Joe find Dan's rifle and six-gun. They're probably in pieces, trampled into the dirt, but he asked 'em to find them, if they could."

"Sure, Cap'n," Ken answered. "C'mon, Nate. Those buffalo broke up the wagon pretty bad, so we won't have any trouble findin' what you need."

It only took Nate and Ken a few moments to find the right sized pieces to splint George's leg. One was lying on the ground, where it had been splintered off, and they pried a second from the tail gate.

"Thanks," Nate said. "These'll do."

"Don't mention it," Ken answered. "Just tell George to heal up as quick as he can. With him laid up, Dakota's gonna have to be the cook, and whatever he makes comes out downright inedible. His bacon's tougher than the shoes he pulls off the horses, his biscuits are like rocks, and his coffee tastes like swamp water. The whole company'll be down with bellyaches and the trots until George gets better."

"I'll tell him," Nate said, with a laugh. "Don't know if there's much he can do about it, but I'll tell him."

****

"Nate, I'm glad to see you got back so soon," Jim said,

once Nate returned. "I've still got three more men to treat, once I'm done with George. Nothing major, Tom's got a sprained ankle, Dakota and Larry some bad bumps, but they still need to be taken care of."

"I told you I wouldn't be long," Nate answered. "Are these all right?"

"They'll do just fine," Jim told him. "Put 'em down alongside George. There's no point puttin' this off any longer. George, I'm gonna pull those bones back in place now. Are you ready?"

"I reckon it don't matter whether I'm ready or not," George said. "It's gotta be done, so you might as well get at it."

"Okay. Nate," Jim said. "I'll need you to hold George's leg still, while I yank the bottom back into place. You'll have to keep it from movin', as much as possible. I also want you to hold George down and keep him from movin', at the same time. The best way to do that is sit on him, just below his hips, grasp his leg, put a hand on each side, a few inches below the knee, and push down hard when I pull. Think you can do that?"

"From what I've seen of Nate, he's always pullin' someone's leg," George said, before Nate could answer.

"Just stuff that bandanna in your mouth, will you, George?" Jim told him. "Nate, can you handle this?"

"I'll manage," Nate said.

"Good. Time to get this done."

Nate got in position and took hold of George's leg, while Jim gripped it six inches above the ankle.

"All right, George?" Jim asked. George nodded.

"Here goes." With a sharp tug, Jim pulled the broken bones back into place. They snapped back with an audible crack. Even with the bandanna in his mouth, George yelled with the pain, then passed out. Nate, himself, got a little queasy, but swallowed hard, and managed to keep his stomach in check.

"It's better that he did lose consciousness," Jim told Nate. "That way, he won't feel anythin' while we finish workin' on him. Hand me those splints."

Nate handed the chuck wagon pieces to Jim, who placed one on each side of George's leg to measure them.

"You chose good," he said. "These are just about the perfect fit."

"Ken helped me find 'em," Nate answered.

"Remind me to thank him," Jim said. "Now, watch while I do this."

Jim took the blanket and cut several strips from it. He used the remainder to wrap around George's leg, then placed a splint on each side. He used the strips to tie those in place, except for two. Those, he used to bind George's pants leg, once it was rolled back down, over the splints.

"There's a couple of reasons to pad a broken limb before you splint it," he explained. "First, it's for the man's comfort. It'll keep the splints or bindings from pressin' on the limb, which could lead to sores, mebbe even gangrene if the sores got bad enough. Second, paddin' the limb helps protect it against bumps and bruises. Third, it helps keep the limb warm. I realize that sounds silly in this heat, but an injured limb can get chilled, no matter how hot the weather is.

"It also helps make certain the splints aren't too tight. You want to make certain they're tight enough the limb can't move, but not so tight they cut off its circulation. The padding helps protect against that. Of course, if you don't have anythin' you can use for padding, you splint anyway.

"I'll remove George's splints and the padding every day for a week or so, just to check the leg, to make certain it hasn't gotten gangrenous. That's about all we can do here for now. I won't need your help with the other men.

"Why don't you go check on your cayuse? I know you're

worried about him. I see Phil and Jeb comin' back. Looks like they've rounded up the horses, so Phil should be with you right quick."

"All right. And thanks for the lesson," Nate said.

"No, thank you for helpin' out. You did just fine. Now, go take care of that horse."

****

Larry Cannon had taken charge of the horse herd. He nodded to Nate when he hurried up.

"Your sorrel's right over there, son," he said. "I took a quick look at him. He's sore, that's for certain, but I couldn't see anythin' obvious. I don't think whatever's botherin' him is too serious. Phil can give you a better idea, once he's turned the remuda in with this bunch."

"Thanks, Larry," Nate said. He whistled. Big Red walked over to him, still limping. He nuzzled Nate's hand.

"I don't have any biscuits right now, Red." Nate patted the horse's shoulder. "I'll try'n find you one in a bit. Right now, we need to see how bad you're hurt." He stayed with Red, talking to him soothingly and comforting him, until Phil approached.

"Red's still limping, Phil," Nate said.

"I figured he would be. A horse don't usually heal up in just a few minutes. I'm just glad I got back sooner than I figured. Jeb and I got every one of the runaways back," he said to Nate. "We got lucky. They didn't scatter all over half of Texas. Now, let me take a look at your bronc. Walk him out for me, will you? Away from me, then toward me."

"Sure." Nate picked up Red's reins, led him away from Phil, then back to him.

"Good, good," Phil said. "Now, trot him out. Same way."

Nate repeated his actions, this time at a trot.

"All right," Phil said, once they were back at his side. "Red's definitely off on his right front. The question is, why? Lemme get a better look. You hold him, and don't let him jump around on me while I check that leg."

"Sure."

While Nate held Red, Phil ran a hand over his right front leg, looking for any signs of injury.

"So far, so good," he said, straightening himself up, then arching his back to work out a kink. "I don't see any lumps, and don't feel any, either. So it appears Red didn't bow a tendon, or tear a ligament or somethin'. And it sure ain't a broken bone, or he wouldn't be placin' any weight on that foot. Now, I'm gonna check his hoof."

Phil picked up Red's foot and examined it closely.

"No pebble stuck in there, and no bruises that I can see," Phil said, as he dropped the foot. "Lemme see what else it might be."

He ran his hand slowly down Red's neck, then his shoulder. When he reached that, the horse flinched, then shied away from Phil's touch. He nickered.

"Ah. There it is," Phil said.

"There what is?" Nate asked, his voice worried. "What's wrong with him?"

"It's actually good news, considerin'," Phil said. "Red must've strained a muscle in his shoulder. A little rest, and he should be good as new, before you know it. Of course, that means you won't be ridin' him for a while. You'll have to choose one of the spare mounts from the remuda. But your horse will be just fine. I've got some liniment in my saddlebags we can rub on that shoulder. It'll help him feel better, and also help him heal faster."

"*Muchas gracias*, Phil," Nate said. "I'm obliged."

"*Por nada*," Phil answered. "Glad to do it. And you're pickin' up Mexican real fast, kid. You're soundin' more and more like a native Texan every day. Now, let's go see if Cap'n Quincy needs our help. After that, we'll come back and rub down Red's shoulder."

****

The men working on uprighting and salvaging the chuck wagon had just completed their work by the time Phil finished checking Big Red. Bob and Hoot had also picked up the tents and supplies lost from the pack mules, and returned. Captain Quincy had gathered all of the men around him. Nate and Phil joined them.

"Nate, Phil, you're just in time to hear what I have to say," he said, then took a drag on his cigarette and tossed the butt aside. "First, the chuck wagon took quite a beatin', but it's repairable, without too much trouble. Fortunately, none of the wheels were broken, and neither of the axles got busted. A couple of hours with hammer and nails and it will be ready to go. That's the good news.

"The bad news is, we lost quite a bit of our supplies, including some of Jim's medicines, most of our foodstuffs, and all of our water. All four barrels were busted wide open when the wagon crashed. Now, Percy's going to scout ahead of us, and search for water. As all of you know, if anyone can locate a waterhole, Percy can. However, the last good source of water in these parts is the Pecos River, and we've already left that quite a few miles behind us.

"This territory is mighty dry country in the best of times, and it's been in a dry spell for quite a while now. That means the odds of Percy findin' any water at all, except mebbe a couple of mud holes, are really slim. We'll have to rely on whatever cactus we can find to cut open for liquid, and whatever's left in our canteens. We'll need to save at least some of that for the horses, and also make certain there's as much as possible kept aside for George and Dan. We could well be lookin' at five days without water, and very little food, until we reach Fort Stockton. We're dang lucky Dan and Percy shot a couple of those buffalo, or we'd go even hungrier."

"Why not send a couple of men ahead to Fort Stockton,

then have 'em bring some water back for us?" Nate suggested.

"If I thought they had any chance at all of makin' it, I'd do exactly that," Quincy answered. "But, just to try it, we'd have to give them what little water we have, and even then, there's no guarantee they'd get through. We're better off stickin' together.

"We'll spend the night here, make the repairs to the wagon, then light out at sunup. I'm not gonna sugar coat things for you. This will be a mighty tough trip, but most of us have faced tougher. We'll get through this, with the help of each other, and the Lord.

"My suggestion for tonight is get as much rest as you can. There's just one other thing. We'll need a driver for the wagon, since George is laid up. Nate, I know George has taught you a little about drivin' a team, but you're not quite experienced enough yet to take on the job. Joe, since you rode shotgun for the Butterfield Stage, you know how to handle a team in a pinch. I'm handin' drivin' the wagon to you. I also want one man to ride along with you, to keep an eye on George and Dan. Nate, I know your horse is hurt. How bad off is he?"

"Phil says Red'll be all right, but I shouldn't ride him for a few days," Nate answered.

"That's right, Cap'n," Phil added. "Nate's horse strained his shoulder. He'll be able to keep up just fine, especially since we won't be travelin' all that fast, but he shouldn't have to take any weight for a while, I'd say at least until we reach Fort Stockton."

"Okay, then that's settled. Nate, you'll ride along with Joe. You won't mind, will you?"

"Not at all, Cap'n," Nate said. "I don't imagine it would make any difference if I did, would it?"

"Probably not, unless someone else volunteered, or if you gave me a good reason why you shouldn't. Besides, most of the other men would gladly trade places with you. They'd love the chance to ride in the wagon, nice and easy, and be out of the saddle for a spell."

"There's no reason that I can think of. I'll be happy to watch Dan and George."

"Good. Now, you men who are fixin' the wagon, get at it. The rest of you, get some shut-eye."

2

The Rangers began to break camp while the gray light of the false dawn was just brightening the eastern horizon. The men ate a meager breakfast, washed down with a few sips of water. The horses were given short drinks from their riders' hats, the animals in the remuda also watered, then the horses were saddled and bridled.

Makeshift beds had been rigged up in the chuck wagon for George and Dan, pieces of canvas which had been torn from its cover by the stampeding buffalo slung as hammocks for the two injured men. Those beds would sway as the wagon jounced along, but would protect George and Dan from the worst of the bouncing. After they were helped into the wagon, they stretched out on the beds, then were covered lightly with thin blankets. The canvas cover had been patched together as much as possible, so it would still provide them at least some protection from the blistering Texas sun. Once they were settled, Joe took his place on the driver's seat. Nate piled some folded blankets just behind him, between George and Dan, then sat down, facing backward, and braced himself against the front boards.

"Are you ready to move out, Joe?" Captain Quincy asked. To keep the injured men out of as much dust as possible, the wagon would travel right behind the captain, Lieutenant Berkeley, and Jeb Rollins.

"I sure am," Joe answered.

"Nate, are you all set?"

"I'm all set, Cap'n."

"Dan, George, are you boys comfortable?"

"I'm as comfortable as I can be, under the circumstances," Dan answered.

"I'm as snug as a bug in a rug," George said. "Just need my Rosita and a bottle of whiskey and I'd be plumb tickled."

"Good. Nate, if either one of those two show any sign somethin' is wrong, you holler out, hear me?" Quincy said.

"I'll do just that," Nate assured him.

"Good. Then it's high time we got movin'." With a wave of his hand, Quincy started the men into motion.

****

Quincy maintained a slow, but steady, pace for the morning, knowing that it would conserve the men's and horses' strength, and keep them a little less thirsty, than traveling faster than a walk. As the sun rose higher in the sky, it beat down mercilessly on the Rangers. Not even the wispiest cloud appeared in the sky to provide at least a bit of shade. A brisk breeze sprang up, but it provided little relief.

The air was so dry the men couldn't even work up a decent sweat, what little perspiration that might have cooled them, at least a touch, instantly evaporating. It took all the willpower they had to keep from opening their canteens and downing the contents in a few quick swallows. The horses and mules were just as miserable. They plodded along, sweat coating their hides with foam, heads hung low, barely lifting their hooves. Just before noon, the captain called a short break.

"I sure hope Percy finds some water, Cap'n," Jeb said to Quincy. "Either that, or we'd better hope a storm blows up. I don't think we can make it to Fort Stockton with what little we have."

Percy had ridden on ahead as soon as they had broken

JAMES J. GRIFFIN

camp, to search for a spring, creek, or any possible source of potable water.

Quincy glanced up at the cloudless, deep blue sky, thumbed back his Stetson, and shook his head.

"I'd say there's no chance of a storm," he said. "There's not any sign of one, at all. There's no moisture in the wind, and it doesn't seem like any clouds are attemptin' to build up. Besides, it's kinda late in the year for thunderstorms. We're just about at the end of the season. It's gettin' almighty close to fall; in fact, it's just a couple of weeks off. My guess is our only chance of findin' water is Percy. We'll just have to keep on goin' and hope he comes across some. We'll rest for thirty minutes, then move on."

Phil Knight rode up. "You sent for me, Cap'n?" he asked.

"Yes, Phil, I did. Our situation is really desperate. If Percy doesn't find any water, you may well have to pick out a couple of animals from the remuda to kill for food. Their meat will at least give us some nourishment, and a bit of moisture."

"Beggin' your pardon, Cap'n, but you'll have to kill me before you'll be allowed to slit the throats of any of those horses or mules," Phil replied. "It ain't their fault we're in this fix. Matter of fact, it's *us* to blame for gettin' *them* into it. No one touches those broncs."

"I'm sorry, but if it comes down to a choice between the horses or the men surviving, there really isn't one," Quincy said. "We'll have to sacrifice some of the horses."

"Not if I can do anythin' to stop you," Phil snapped. He turned Parker and spurred him into a lope, heading back to the remuda.

"Phil means just what he said, Cap'n," Jeb said.

"I know it," Quincy answered. "Here's prayin' to God it doesn't come to that."

****

After the rest, the Rangers resumed their westward trek. They had gone about four miles when a horse and rider appeared.

"Someone up ahead, Cap'n," Bob said. He took his field glasses from his saddlebags, and put them to his eyes for a closer look.

"Well, Bob?" Quincy asked, as his lieutenant studied the oncoming rider. "Can you make out who it is?"

"Yep. It's Percy. Let's hope he's found us some water."

A few moments later, Percy rode up to them, and reined in his horse.

"Afternoon, Cap'n, Lieutenant," he said.

"Never mind the pleasantries, Percy," Quincy said. "Did you come across any water? We're gettin' pretty desperate. George and Dan got the last of our water three-four hours ago."

"I'm not sure," Percy answered. "I didn't see any, for certain, but a few miles ahead there is a thin line of greenery off to the northwest, probably along a creek bed. I'd doubt it's any sort of large trees that would indicate plenty of water, like cottonwoods or cypresses. It's more likely some mesquite and scrub willows. I'd say a couple miles off the trail. It could be there's some water, or it could be just a whole lotta damp sand.

"It'd be a bit of a detour, but it might be worthwhile. It's up to you, Cap'n, whether you want to chance it, or just keep pushin' on and hope for the best. Before you make your decision, since the sign wasn't all that good, I need to tell you instead of checking the spot out more closely, I decided to keep lookin' for a more likely place. I scouted ahead ten miles past where I spotted that vegetation, and found no sign of water at all."

"That's a mighty quick pace in this heat, Percy," Bob said. "How'd you manage it?"

Percy leaned forward in his saddle and patted his wiry

pinto's neck. "Wind Runner, here, is an Indian pony. He can go for days with just a few snatches of grass, and hardly any water. He held up just fine, and he's still got some more miles in him."

"Percy, what do you think the odds are there really is water where you spotted that greenery?" Quincy asked.

Percy shrugged. "I'd say fifty-fifty, maybe a bit less."

"What would you do if you were in charge of this outfit?"

"I'd take the chance and head for that creek bed."

"Then that's what we'll do," Quincy decided. "Jeb, pass the word along Percy might've found some water."

"I'll do just that," Jeb said. He turned Dudley and started to ride back along the column of Rangers.

"Cap'n, there is just one more thing I should mention before we head for that creek bed," Percy said, once Jeb was out of earshot. He kept his voice low, so none of the other men could overhear what he was about to say.

"What is it, Percy?"

"You're about to see why those buffalo stampeded. You won't be happy, not one bit. It's not a pretty sight."

****

"How much farther until we reach that place you're talkin' about, Percy?" Quincy asked the scout, two hours later.

"We're just about there," Percy answered. "If you look real hard, you can barely make out a bit of green, over to the right about thirty degrees. It's close to two-and-a-half miles off. From what I could see, the terrain between this trail and what I hope is some water is mighty rough. However, there's a shallow dry wash which cuts off toward the spot we're headed for, which should make the crossing at least a bit easier. We'll be at the turn in a short while."

Quincy lifted his hand to further shield his eyes from the sun. He squinted as he attempted to see the vegetation

Percy had found. He finally made out what appeared to be a thin ribbon of green, lightly coloring the horizon.

"It sure doesn't look like much," he said, "But as the saying goes, beggars can't be choosers. Our situation is gettin' pretty desperate. We'll last mebbe another day or so if we don't come up with some water soon, and the horses are just about played out from thirst. We'll have to chance it."

****

"I sure hope Percy's right about there bein' some water ahead, Hoot," Nate said to his partner, as Hoot rode alongside the wagon. Hoot was leading Red, and both his dun and Nate's sorrel had their heads hung low. Red was still saddled and bridled, so Nate's gear didn't have to be stowed in the wagon or packed on one of the mules. Their mounts, as well as all the Rangers' horses, were gaunt from lack of water, their ribs hollow-appearing and their flanks caved in. "My mouth feels like it's full of cotton, and my tongue's swollen so big I can hardly swallow, it seems like. But it's not me I'm worried about. It's Red. Lookin' at him, between his hurt shoulder and not havin' any water, I don't think he's got too much left in him. He needs a drink, bad."

"I hear you, pard," Hoot answered. "I ain't had a drink in so long I think my guts are all shriveled up, and my plumbin's dried up. Now, me'n Dusty have been on some mighty dry trails before, but this one's the worst I can recall. I've never seen him so thinned out from lack of water. And he's more used to doin' without it than your horse. If Dusty's in this bad a shape, poor Red must really be sufferin'. But I wouldn't get overly worried... at least, not yet. As long as Percy's been with the company, he's always managed to find water, just when everyone else has given up. Your horse'll be drinkin' his fill pretty soon. Only be sure to remember, when we do get to water, don't let him drink too fast, or too much. Only let him have a little bit. If he drinks too much, he's liable to colic, or founder. Either one of those things could kill him. So no matter how much he fights you, limit his water."

"Thanks for the advice," Nate said. "I never would have thought about that. I would've let Red drink until his belly just about busted, if you hadn't warned me not to."

"If I hadn't, you can bet your hat one of the other boys would have stopped you from lettin' him have too much," Hoot answered. "Hey, what's that sound? You hear it?"

"I don't hear anythin' but the horses' hooves cloppin', and Ken grousin' about somethin' or other," Nate said. "How about you, Joe?"

"I don't hear a thing, except you two yappin'," Joe answered. "George? Dan? Either of you hear anythin'?"

"Just the wagon creakin', and Dan's belly rumblin'," George said.

"That ain't my belly," Dan retorted. "That's the wagon springs complainin' every time Joe hits a chuckhole, and he ain't missed one yet."

"No, I mean it. I hear somethin'," Hoot insisted. "Just keep still and listen. It's kind of a buzzin' noise."

The four other men strained to hear whatever Hoot's ears had detected. Dan was the first to also catch the sound.

"Wait a minute. I hear what you're talkin' about, Hoot. What the devil is that?" he said.

"I dunno," Hoot answered. "I've never heard anythin' like it before."

"Now I hear it, too," Nate added. "It sounds like a couple thousand or so bees all stirred up because someone poked a stick into their hive. And it's gettin' louder."

"Percy already rode through here," Joe said. "Mebbe he knows what it is. Let's ask him."

Before Joe could call to Percy, the scout leaned over in his saddle and said something, softly, to Captain Quincy. In turn, Quincy raised his hand and ordered the men to stop. He turned to face them.

"Boys," he said. "We're gettin' closer to where Percy thinks there might be some water. But he's got somethin' to warn y'all about before we go any farther. Percy..."

"*Gracias*, Cap'n. Men, I know none of you will ever forget that buffalo stampede we managed to survive. While I was lookin' for water, I discovered what scared those buffs so badly. They were bein' hunted. Just ahead is what the hunters left of a whole passel of animals. The scavengers have already been at 'em, and picked some of them clean to the bone. However, those men killed so many buffalo even the buzzards, coyotes, and other critters couldn't eat the leavin's, at least not all at once. And of course, bein' white hunters, they just took the hides and some of the prime meat, then left the rest to rot. So, there's a lot of decayin' carcasses we've got to get by in order to reach the water, which I think is less'n a half mile away now. I don't need to tell you there'll be one heckuva stench. I'd recommend you bring your bandannas up over your noses, to at least keep out some of the smell. I'd take a spare one and tie it over your horse's nose, also. In fact, some of you might have to also blindfold your cayuse, if he gets spooked. Besides the smell, we'll be stirrin' up whatever scavengers are still workin' on those carcasses."

"Is that where the buzzin's comin' from, Percy?" Nate asked.

"You beat me to it," Percy answered. "I was just about to tell you that buzzin's from thousands of flies, feedin' on those dead buffalo. Between the smell of decay and blood, the sight of the carcasses, and the critters we disturb, I expect the horses are gonna act up somethin' fierce. Those flies are probably gonna swarm us. You can't expect any horse to ride through something like that and not get worried, even the most hardened battle horse. So all of you need to hold on tight, and keep your broncs under control. Don't hesitate for one minute to blindfold any animal you think needs it. As far as the pace, we'll probably ride through at a trot. That'll be fast enough so the horses won't have too much time to think about what we're puttin' 'em through, but not so fast they'll spook, and start a runaway. That could change, depending on exactly how they react. Nate, I think it would be best if you got outta that wagon and rode your horse, until we got out of this spot. It won't hurt him to be ridden for a short way. In fact, if he gets too nervous, it'll be better if you're on his back to calm him down. That just might keep him from hurtin' himself worse."

"Okay," Nate said. He clambered out of the wagon, took Red's reins from Hoot, and pulled himself into the saddle.

"What about the ones in the remuda?" Hoot asked, once Nate was mounted.

"They could be a problem," Percy admitted. "However, if the rest of us get through, they'll most likely follow. They won't want to be left behind. And Phil's the best there is when it comes to keepin' a horse herd bunched. I'm not overly worried about them. Cap'n, that's all I've got to say."

"Thanks, Percy." Quincy said. "Men," he continued. "I can't add anything to what Percy just told you. We'll take a minute so you can cover your mouths and noses, and your horses'. Then, we'll head for that water."

"If there is any," Jeb mumbled, under his breath.

****

As they approached what all of the men hoped would be a source of sweet water, Hoot pointed to several dark mounds, lying on the ground a short distance ahead. He pulled down his bandanna for a moment, to speak to Nate.

"I reckon those are the first of the dead buffalo Percy was talkin' about, Nate," he said. "Seems like there's still some buzzards workin' on the carcasses, from what I can see. They'll sure raise a squawk when we ride through there. You might need everythin' you have to keep Red under control. I know I'll have one devil of a time keepin' Sandy from panickin', tossin' me, and runnin' off. And I've been ridin' half-broke broncs a lot longer'n you have."

Nate pulled down his own bandanna before replying.

"I think Big Red'll do all right. At least, I sure hope so. I guess we're about to find out how good a horse he really is...and how good a rider I'm turnin' out to be."

He patted Red's neck, to reassure the big sorrel. "It's gonna be all right, Red," he whispered to him.

Some of the horses, rattled by the constant buzzing of thousands of insects, and the horrific odor drifting to their sensitive nostrils, were already tossing their heads, prancing nervously, and snorting protests as the Rangers drew nearer the killing field. When several buzzards, disturbed from their grisly feast by the approaching riders, squawked in anger and flapped slowly into the air, Tom's horse jumped sideways, nearly spilling his rider. Ken's horse leapt straight in the air, came down stiff-legged, and spun a half-circle, attempting to run back the direction from which he'd come. It took all their riders' efforts to bring the horses back under control. Phil was barely able to keep the remuda bunched, swinging Parker from one side to the other to keep the animals together.

Now, the extent of the carnage was becoming clear, as the men rode past the dead buffalo. There were at least one hundred skinned carcasses lying scattered between the trail and the line of greener vegetation, which did indeed mark a shallow creek bed. Flies by the hundreds rose into the air as the riders went past, many of them landing on the horses and biting, sending them into a frenzy of kicking and switching their tails. Almost every horse was ready to bolt, given the chance. Red was dancing sideways, fighting Nate's every effort to keep him moving forward, while Dusty would rear high, paw at the air, then come back down on all fours, shaking violently in a futile effort to rid himself of the tormenting insects. Adding to their fear was the sight of so many bloody carcasses, the overpowering smell, and the taut nerves of their riders. Only Jeb's Dudley, and Percy's Wind Runner, seemed unperturbed by the situation.

The men themselves, despite being used to the gory results of Indian attacks, outlaw raids, and cattle stampedes, were also having great difficulty keeping what little contents they had in their stomachs down. The almost unbearable stench was nauseating, the combination of it, the heat, and the pitching horses also headache-inducing for many of the men.

"We're gonna move a little faster, to try and get past this mess before the horses really panic," Percy called. "Keep up with me." He slapped a fly on Wind Runner's neck, then put him into a fast trot.

Still fighting their horses, the rest of the men followed. A few moments later, they reached the meager shelter of the scrub brush lining the creek bed. They crashed through the brush, which offered at least some protection from the flies. Percy pulled his horse to a stop, then waited while the other horses were settled, and the mules pulling the wagon calmed.

"I don't see any water, Percy," Captain Quincy said. "And the sand doesn't even look damp enough that we'd find any by diggin' for it."

Percy indicated a clump of mesquite and dwarf cottonwoods about a hundred yards ahead.

"I'd say that's a waterhole, just up there," he said. "Let's find out."

"What about any bushwhackers who might be waitin' for us? We'd better send one or two men to scout that out first," Larry suggested.

"I don't reckon we'll have to worry about anyone waitin' to drygulch us," Percy answered. "Not with all those rottin' buffalo back there. I doubt anyone'd think someone worth robbin' would come along, not through that. Let's go."

Percy heeled his pinto into a walk, with Captain Quincy alongside him, the rest of the men strung out behind. A slight breeze brought the scent of water to the horses' nostrils. They forgot the fear they'd had, instead fighting to yank the reins from their riders' hands and dash headlong for the waterhole.

"Keep those animals in check," Percy urged. "Don't let any of 'em get to water until I make certain it's safe. Just wait here. Cap'n Dan and I will ride on ahead."

He and Captain Quincy covered the remaining distance at a slow jogtrot. When they pushed their way through the thicker brush surrounding the waterhole, Percy jerked Wind Runner to a halt, and yanked him back, before he could attempt to dip his muzzle in the shallow pool. He cursed, while Captain Quincy added a string of oaths of his own, for good measure.

"Those..." Percy exclaimed. "There was no reason for 'em to do this. Not knowin' there's no other water for miles around. This is a low down, dirty trick."

Several dead buffalo were sprawled on the banks of the waterhole. Three more lay in the water itself, their blood tinging it pink, fouling it and making it undrinkable.

"You're right, Percy," Quincy answered. "Those hombres had to know they were signin' a death sentence for anyone expectin' to get water here. There's no excuse for it. Those rotten, miserable, sons..."

"Includin' us," Percy said. "This water won't be fit to drink for a long time, if ever again."

"Quite possibly," Quincy answered. He shrugged. "Well, there's nothin' we can do about it. Let's go back and break the news to the others. Then, we'll keep pushin' on, and hope by some miracle we stumble across some water. That's all we can do."

They turned their horses and headed back to the waiting men, who watched expectantly as they approached, their eyes bright with hope. Seeing the downcast expressions on Percy's and Quincy's faces, they instantly realized whatever hope they had of finding water had been dashed.

"Well, Cap'n, is there any water at all?" Lieutenant Bob asked, knowing what the answer would be even before posing the question.

"Oh, there's water all right. Plenty of it. A nice, big pool," Quincy answered. "But those buffalo hunters killed some animals right at the waterhole, and left the carcasses in it. The water's been poisoned. It's not fit to drink. We're gonna have to move on, and hope the Good Lord guides us to some water."

His news brought a general grumbling from the men, as well as several not very complimentary comments about the buffalo hunters' ancestry. Jim Kelly summed up the feelings of all when he said, "I'd rather the Lord guide us to those sidewinders, so we could show 'em what happens to men who deliberately poison waterholes in this territory."

"I'd imagine everyone agrees with you, Jim, but complainin' isn't gonna help our situation. We can't stay here, that's for certain. However, we can't travel much further, in this heat. We'll ride just far enough to get away from here, to put the stink and flies behind us. Soon as we've done that, we'll try and find at least a bit of shade, but even if we don't, we'll stop for the remainder of the day, get some rest, then resume travelin' after the sun goes down, and it cools off a bit. The moon's almost full, so that'll make for easy ridin, most of the night."

"And I'm gonna ride out ahead, an hour or so before sundown, to search for water again," Percy added. "There has to be some out there, somewhere."

"So there you have it," Quincy said. "We push on."

Nate was given a moment to dismount, then climb back into the wagon. Once he was settled, the Rangers resumed their trek.

****

A mile later, Captain Quincy once again called a halt. Less than a quarter-mile ahead was a small, steep sided mesa.

"We'll stop just ahead, alongside that mesa," he ordered. "As the afternoon gets later and the sun gets lower, it'll cast a pretty good shadow, which will provide us some shade. It looks like there might even be a little dried-up grass for the horses to nibble on."

"It ain't gonna help us all that much if we don't find some water, and right quick," Dakota muttered.

"We're all aware of that," Quincy answered. "However, if we don't stop for a spell, we won't make it through the rest of the day. Mebbe, with a fresh start in the cool of the evenin', we'll make it to water. In the meantime, take care of your horses, then get some rest."

He put Bailey into a slow walk, the most he could ask from his worn-out horse. Fifteen minutes later, they reached the mesa. The men dismounted. Dan and George were helped from the wagon, then placed underneath it, where they would be protected from the sun. The horses were untacked, the mules pulling the wagon unhitched, and the pack mules relieved of their burdens. They were brushed, and left to pick at whatever grass they could find. Most of the men stretched out wherever they could.

Jim, with Nate watching, examined the two injured

men.

"You're both doin' all right, considerin'," he told them, once he was done. "Of course, it don't help none you haven't had any water. Nate'n I'll stick here, just in case you need anythin'." He settled against one of the wagon's wheels, Nate against another.

Percy, Jeb, and Hoot, having finished caring for their horses, wandered over. They hunkered alongside the wagon.

"How're these boys doin', Jim?" Percy asked.

"Not all that badly," Jim answered. "It's a real shame what those hunters did, poisonin' that waterhole. Really left us in a bad fix."

"We'll be in even deeper trouble right quick, thanks to them," Hoot added.

"Men like that have no conscience," Jeb said. "They only care about themselves, and the heck with everyone else. They killed those animals only for the hides, and a little of the meat. Look at how much meat they left behind, to rot in the sun. Men like those make my blood boil."

"I've been wonderin' about that," Nate said. "Why would they waste so much?"

"I'll answer that," Percy said. His eyes glittered with anger. "Nate, there used to be more buffalo roamin' the prairies than you could count. One herd could be so large, with so many animals, it would take two or three days to pass a spot. And many of us Indians followed the buffalo as they migrated. Buffalo provided food for our bellies, hides for our tipis, blankets for our beds, clothes for our bodies, even grease and tallow. Their bones were made into tools, arrowheads, even needles. Sinew was worked into thread. Not one part of the animal wasn't used, not one bit wasted. And, we only killed as many as we needed to survive. In fact, the buffalo is considered sacred by the Indian. We believed the buffalo would be with us forever...until the white man arrived."

He hesitated. "Maybe you don't want to hear this, Nate. I'm real bitter about this subject."

"You're wrong, Percy. I sure do," Nate answered. "Go ahead."

"Okay. Once the railroads started building across the continent, they brought in hunters to shoot buffalo, first to provide meat for the workers, then later just for sport. They killed animals by the thousands.

"Later, the so-called professional hunters moved in. They hunt almost only for the hides, because buffalo robes and coats are fashionable back East. As you just saw, they don't care about how many animals they kill, or how much goes to waste. They shoot as many as they can, skin them, perhaps take some of the meat, then move on to kill more. They don't realize, or don't give a da- uh, darn, that they are rapidly killing off the buffalo.

"The once vast herds are rapidly being depleted. Already, I understand hunters have to travel farther and farther to look for fewer and fewer animals. Of course, with the buffalo disappearing, and most Indians confined to reservations, my people are becoming ever more dependent on Government handouts...help which quite often never reaches the people it's intended for, but which instead is diverted by dishonest Indian agents for their own gain.

"Mark my words, it won't be too many days distant before the buffalo is completely wiped out. That won't only be a tragedy for the Indian, but also the white man. Wolves and mountain lions, which prey on the buffalo, will begin to starve, and will turn to attacking livestock, especially the young. If they are hungry enough, they could even start killing humans, all because of shortsighted men and their greed."

"I never would've guessed," Nate admitted. "From what I've heard and read, there were plenty of buffalo. Now, you tell me there aren't."

"Percy's right," Jeb said. "You can ride over some places on the plains where you can see the bleached bones of buffalo for miles. And nobody's gonna do anythin' about it. There's too much profit to be made from the buffalo. They'll be gone, and it will be everyone's loss."

"I hate to point this out," Jim said, "but if we don't find some water, we'll all be extinct long before the buffalo...in fact, in the next few days. Now, as the company surgeon, or the closest thing to one we've got, I'm tellin' you to get some rest. That'll help conserve your strength, at least a little. I'd advise drinkin' your own urine, to get a little moisture, but I'd imagine every one of you has dried up."

Nate grimaced.

"You'd actually expect us to drink our own pee, Jim?"

"Out here, a man has to do whatever he can to survive," Jim explained. "When you're desperate enough, you'll do it, too. I've done it, and it's saved my life. Some other men I know, too. It ain't pleasant, but it sure beats the alternative, dyin' of thirst. But I wouldn't worry too much. We're not licked, at least not quite yet."

"Jim's right, Nate," Jeb added, trying to reassure the young, and still learning, Ranger. "We've been in worse fixes. We'll get through this one, too. So take Jim's advice and try'n get a little shut-eye."

"You heard the man, pardner. Let's go," Hoot said.

****

Nate and Hoot found a spot alongside some rocks which had tumbled from the mesa, and which provided at least a bit of shade. Despite their hunger and thirst, both soon fell asleep. Sometime while they were dozing, Percy rode out, once again searching for water.

Just before sundown, they were awakened by the shouting of Tom, who had been posted as sentry.

"Percy's comin' back," he yelled. "Looks like he might've come across somethin'."

Percy was returning at a gallop. When he reached the camp, everyone had awakened. They gathered around him. A dead pronghorn was draped over Wind Runner's rump.

"Did you find any water?" Captain Quincy asked.

"No luck there, but at least I got somethin' that'll help," Percy answered. "I shot this buck a couple miles back. It'll give us fresh meat, and moisture besides."

"All right. Good work, Percy," Quincy said. "Jeb, Ken, get that pronghorn down, and start butcherin' it."

"You want me to start lookin' for some firewood, Cap'n?" Nate asked.

"We won't be cookin' this animal," Quincy said. "We'll eat it raw. That's how we'll get some of the moisture we need to keep on goin'."

"Raw?" Nate echoed.

"That's right, raw," Jeb confirmed. "Percy probably just saved all of our lives by downin' this pronghorn."

He and Ken pulled the pronghorn off Wind Runner, took out their Bowie knives, and began carving chunks of meat from it. The first pieces were given to George and Dan. When Nate received his, he screwed up his face in distaste.

"I can't eat this, Hoot," he said.

"You have to," Hoot answered. "You need the meat, and the moisture. Sure, it ain't gonna taste all that good, but it'll keep you goin'. And raw like it is, the meat'll slide down your gullet real easy. It'll probably make you a bit sick, but you've got to keep it down, if you possibly can."

"I dunno," Nate said. He looked at the bloody hunk of meat he held. "I just don't know."

"Watch me," Hoot said. He bit a large piece off the meat he held, and began chewing. Blood ran down his chin and dripped onto his shirtfront. "See, nothin' to it. Give it a try."

"You'd better eat that, Nate," Lieutenant Berkeley advised him. "It just might keep you alive."

"All right, Bob." Nate gulped, lifted the piece of pronghorn to his mouth, took a bite, and began chewing. The coppery taste of blood filled his mouth. When he swallowed the first piece, his stomach revolted, churning, its contents threatening to come right back up. Bile rose in his throat. Nate forced it back down, fighting the nausea.

"See, Nate, I told you it wouldn't be all that bad," Hoot said. "Try another bite."

Nate did, tearing off another piece with his front teeth, then chewing the tough, stringy meat. Blood now ran down his chin, leaving streaks on his shirtfront.

"That's showin' some gumption, Nate," Jeb said. "You're doin' just fine."

"Yeah, except he looks like some kind of savage, with the blood all over his face," Hoot said, with a laugh.

"I reckon that pretty much goes for all of us," Jeb answered. Indeed, every man had blood coating his mouth and chin. Some had it smeared on the backs of their hands, or their shirt sleeves, from using those to wipe it off their faces.

Nate had to admit, once he got past the first taste, the meat, while not something he'd want as a regular diet, was somewhat palatable. And he could feel it reviving him, at least a bit. He not only ate the first piece, but two others besides. His belly now full, he leaned back against a rock, with a satisfied sigh.

"Seems like that meat agreed with you after all, Nate," Captain Quincy said. "I know it wasn't your mama's cookin', but it's what you needed. You'll find out more and more that, out here, you'll eat whatever comes your way, if you have to."

"Like the rattlesnake Percy shot, the one that nearly bit me?" Nate said.

"Exactly. Just like that," Quincy answered. "Men," he continued, "We'll rest another hour, to let your supper digest. Be ready to ride ten minutes after that."

****

The Rangers rode out shortly after eight o'clock, and aided by the light of the nearly full moon, traveled until shortly before six in the morning. At that time, Captain Quincy called a halt.

"This is about as far as the horses can go without rest," he said. "We'll spend the day here, then start out again just after sundown."

Once again, the horses and mules were cared for, then turned loose to find whatever grazing they could. Too tired and thirsty to care about eating, most of the men found places to make rough beds and quickly fell asleep.

****

The next day, the sun once again rose brassily in an absolutely cloudless sky. However, by mid-morning, the sky was covered by a thin haze, which lowered and thickened as the morning progressed. By noon, the arid West Texas landscape was covered by a rare fog. Despite the Rangers' fervent hopes and prayers, the fog never developed into a life-sustaining rain, not even a brief shower. However, its moisture did provide some relief for the desperate men, and their animals.

Captain Quincy decided to get on the trail earlier than planned, to take advantage of the cool, damp conditions. Odds were the fog would lift before the day was done, so rather than waiting until dusk, he wanted to cover as much distance as possible before the usual blistering heat returned.

Fortunately, the fog persisted much longer than anyone expected. It was late afternoon before the sun finally burned through it, and the heat started to build, once again.

"We gonna try and hole up for awhile, Cap'n, or keep on pushin'?" Lieutenant Bob asked.

"We'll ride a bit farther, to see if there's somewhere with a bit of shade," Captain Quincy answered. "And just mebbe Percy's found some water."

The Tonkawa scout had once again ridden ahead of the company, searching for any possible remote waterhole.

"I doubt that, Cap'n," Jeb said. "There's Percy comin' now, and he don't look none too happy. In fact, I'd say he's downright mad."

A few minutes later, Percy rode up to them.

"Any luck, Percy?" Quincy asked.

"Only bad, and gettin' worse," Percy answered. "I spotted some wagons, about two miles ahead. Turns out they belonged to buffalo hunters. They were settin' up camp for the night. I'd wager it's the same outfit that caused the stampede which nearly killed us."

"Probably," Quincy agreed. "But that also means they have water. Did you ask 'em if they could spare some?"

Percy shook his head. "I never got close enough to let them see me. I'm not that loco. A lone Indian askin' a bunch of buffalo hunters for help? Once they stopped laughin' their fool heads off, they'd have killed me for certain."

"I'm sorry, Percy," Quincy apologized. "I should've thought of that. I reckon I'm just so thirsty it's fried my brain."

"Mebbe they'll give us some water, Cap'n Dave," Jeb suggested.

"My thoughts exactly. When they see the bad shape we're in, they'll share some," Quincy said.

"I'm not so certain about that," Jeb said. "Most buffalo hunters are downright mean. They ain't gonna be worried about us."

"Even buffalo hunters aren't that ornery, to deny water to dyin' men," Quincy replied. "Jim said George and Dan are gettin' feverish, and need water, bad. They won't last the night otherwise. Neither will some of the other men, nor most of the horses. We'll get some water from those hunters."

Again, Percy shook his head. "I wouldn't count on that. Remember, if this is the same outfit that stampeded the herd back yonder, it's the same one which poisoned the waterhole. They ain't gonna care about anyone but themselves."

"We'll see about that," Quincy said. "Let's move. Jeb, ride back and tell the men we're only going a couple more miles, and, with any luck, they'll be quenching their thirst real soon."

"Right, Cap'n." Jeb sketched a quick salute, then turned Dudley, while Quincy waved the column into motion, once again.

****

Half an hour later, they rode up to the buffalo hunters' camp. There were eight men, and four wagons, piled high with hides. Two water barrels were lashed to the side of one, and several waterskins hung from the others. The hunters watched suspiciously as the Rangers approached. They held their rifles at the ready. As soon as Captain Quincy rode into range, one of the men lifted his gun, a huge single shot .50 caliber Sharps, and leveled it at Quincy's chest.

"I dunno who you boys are, but you'd best keep right on a-goin', less'n you all want bullets through your bellies," he said.

Quincy raised his hands, shoulder high. "Just take it easy, mister," he said. "We're not lookin' for any trouble, nor to try'n steal your hides. I'm Texas Ranger Captain

David Quincy, and these are my men. We're on our way to Fort Stockton. All we're lookin' for is a little water. We lost all of ours when our chuck wagon overturned, and the barrels got smashed. I've got a couple of injured men who won't last the night, if they don't get some water. Same goes for our horses."

Quincy deliberately omitted telling the hunters exactly why the wagon was wrecked. Despite his sincere desire to tell these men exactly what he felt about them, then shoot them down, he held his temper in check. Antagonizing them now would only guarantee they wouldn't give up any of their water.

"Well, ain't that just a real pity?" the hunter said. "Ain't that too bad, boys?" he repeated. The other hunters nodded their agreement.

"Ranger, I'm sorry, but we've only got just enough water for ourselves. We sure can't spare any." He spat out a thick stream of tobacco, most of which dribbled down his thick, matted beard, then smiled, revealing crooked, yellow teeth. He, as were all the hunters in the group, was unkempt, dressed in greasy buckskins, his hair long and tangled.

"Are you the leader of this outfit?" Quincy asked.

"I sure am," the man answered. "Buck Trenton, at your service."

"Well, Mr. Trenton, we're not asking for a lot," Quincy said. "We only need enough for the next two days or so. Surely you can allow us that much. We'd be obliged."

"Ranger, you must be deaf, or just plain thick," Trenton answered. "You ain't gettin' any water from us, and that's my last word. Of course, we do have plenty of corn liquor, but you boys ain't gettin' any of that, either. Now, just get ridin' before we start shootin'."

Quincy could feel the tension in the men behind him, their eagerness to grab for their guns and start shooting. However, the hunters already had their guns out, and the

Rangers were covered. To start a gun battle now would only be a bloodbath... a bloodbath which he and his men would be certain to lose.

"Okay," he said. "But you mind if I ask you one thing before we move on?"

"All right, as long as you make it quick," Trenton agreed.

"Our wagon got wrecked by a herd of stampedin' buffalo, a herd spooked by hunters. The same hunters shot some buffs and left 'em in the only waterhole our scout could find, poisonin' it. Would you by any chance be the same outfit?"

Trenton tossed back his head and laughed.

"Why, Mister Ranger Captain, we sure are. We wasn't takin' any chances someone else could use that water, and mebbe move in on our herds, or steal the hides we took fair and square. Yeah, we poisoned that water."

Quincy finally lost his temper. He let loose a string of curses that made even the hunters blush.

"You about done, Ranger?" Trenton said, when he finished.

"Yep," Quincy said. "But some day there'll be payback for what you've done. Bet your hat on it."

"I ain't wearin' a hat," Trenton retorted. "And if you want to keep yours, get movin', right now, before I blast your head right out from under it."

Quincy shrugged his shoulders. "You heard the hombre," he said to his men. "Let's go."

Every Ranger's stomach muscles were tight, every nerve on edge, as they rode past the hunters. Each man wanted to draw his gun, but each knew it would be foolish to do so. It stuck in their craws, but they all rode past, silently. However, every man also glared at the hunters, daring them to try something. And they twisted in their saddles to look back once they were past, keeping their eyes on the men to make certain they wouldn't shoot them in their backs, until they were out of sight.

"Hoot, those men stink almost as bad as the carcasses they left behind," Nate whispered.

"Buffalo hunters don't exactly smell like honeysuckle and roses," Hoot whispered back. "It's a dirty business. And those hides they've got piled in those wagons smell to high heaven, too. It's sickenin', that's for certain. But, we'll be outta here soon enough."

As the men rode along, most of them grumbled about not doing something to get some water from the hunters. Captain Quincy called a halt and turned to face his angry Rangers.

"Men, I wanted to shoot those hombres down where they stood, just as badly as you did. However, if we'd tried, all that would've done is gotten us all killed. Y'all know that as surely as I do."

"It still frosts me, Cap'n," Carl said.

"Same here," Dakota answered.

"But not as much as it angers me," Percy said. "It's men like those who are causing the extermination of an entire people, my people. That bunch is one I wouldn't mind eating, after they'd died with my bullets in them."

"You'd get stomach poisonin' if you tried," Jeb said. "Those hombres were real filthy, even for buffalo hunters. One bite'd most likely kill you. If their fleas didn't suck all the blood outta you first."

"You're probably right," Percy said. "Sadly, there are too many men like those out here."

"But we're workin' on riddin' Texas of their kind," Quincy said. "Now, we'll ride a couple more miles, then quit for the evening. I figure we'll rest until two in the mornin', and start out again. Let's go."

****

Nate had been sleeping for about three hours when he felt a nudge on his shoulder, and someone softly whispering his name. He opened his eyes to see Jeb Rollins standing over him.

"Jeb. What the..."

"Shhh," Jeb put a warning finger to his lips. "Pull on your boots and gun, and come with me. Real quiet, now. We don't want to wake anyone else. Hurry."

Nate nodded his understanding. He slid from under his blankets, stamped into his boots, jammed his hat on his head, then stood up and buckled his gunbelt around his waist. He followed Jeb to where the horses and mules were picketed. Already there were Hoot, Carl, Percy, and Jim. They were saddling their mounts.

"Jeb, what's goin' on?" Nate asked.

"Nate, keep your voice down," Jeb urged. "You're about to learn Rangers sometimes do what has to be done, and the devil take the hindmost, no matter what the consequences. We're goin' to get us some water."

"From where?"

"From those buffalo hunters, ya idjit," Hoot answered. He held Diablo, the horse which had belonged to Andy Pratt, until the young Ranger was gunned down. He handed the black's lead rope to Nate. "Phil said since you can't ride your horse, take Andy's. He's the fastest one in the remuda. Get him saddled. Your rig's right over there."

"The buffalo hunters?" Nate echoed, as he picked up his saddle and blanket.

"That's right," Jeb confirmed. "You didn't think we'd let 'em get away with what they did to us, did you?"

"I figured they had us over a barrel," Nate said. "Cap'n Dave said there wasn't anythin' we could do."

"What Cap'n Dave said doesn't matter, at least not right now," Jim said. "We need water, that's all there is to it. Dan and George are just about finished. Some of the other men can't last much longer, either. Same for the horses. And the only water around these parts those hunters have. So, we're goin' after it."

"You mean Cap'n Dave doesn't know what we're up to?" Nate said.

"No, he doesn't," Jeb answered. "Not exactly. But he wouldn't be surprised at what we're tryin' to pull. And of course, once we come back with water, he'll know about it."

"In fact, he probably suspects some of us are up to somethin'," Jim added. "But it's better if he and Lieutenant Bob are left outta this, just in case our plan doesn't work."

"That's why I was glad to sign on with the Rangers," Carl added. "I'd heard this here outfit does what needs doin', and worries later about bendin' the rules, as long as the job gets done. Sure looks like I was right."

"And you know why I'm doin' this," Percy said. "It's personal. Perhaps this will bring about at least a little revenge for my people."

"Let's get 'er done," Jeb said. "Everyone saddled?"

"Seems so," Jim said.

"Then mount up. I'll go over the details while we ride. And keep quiet as possible."

****

The six men made it out of camp without disturbing any of the others. As they rode past, Phil, who was guarding the remuda, touched the brim of his Stetson in a silent good luck sign. Jeb waited until they were well out of earshot before explaining his plan.

"Nate and Hoot, your job is to scatter the hunters' horses," he said. "You'll have to ride in a little ahead of us, so be careful. Make certain you don't wake up any of those men before you reach the horses. You'll be liable to catch a bullet if you do. You can be certain those men are crack shots, and those single-shot .50 caliber Sharps they use can blow a hole big as a fist clean through a man at five hundred yards.

"Once you do reach the horses, make as much of a ruckus as you can. That'll bring most, if not all, of the men your way. Soon as we hear the horses runnin' off, me, Jim, Percy, and Carl will move in. We'll latch onto some of the waterskins, then hightail it outta there. Now, you two don't wait for us. Soon as those horses are scattered, you light a shuck for camp. Ride like your horses' tails were afire and the Devil himself was after you. And he might as well be, since the hunters will be on your tails. Don't stop for anythin', no matter what you hear, how much shootin' there is. You got that?"

"I got it, Jeb," Hoot said. Nate nodded his understanding.

"Good. Anyone have any questions?"

"I've got one," Nate said. "Do you think there'll be a guard posted?"

"I doubt it," Jeb said. "Those men ain't worried. They don't imagine anyone'd dare take after 'em."

"Besides, knowing buffalo hunters like I do, I'd imagine they worked on that corn liquor Trenton mentioned before they turned in," Percy said. "They probably got good and drunk. If they did, that works to our advantage."

"But if there is a guard, it'll be your job to take care of him, Hoot," Jeb said. "Don't take any chances. Put a bullet in him before he has the chance to cut you down. Remember what I said about what a .50 caliber slug can do to a man. Now, are there any other questions?"

The only response was silence.

"Good. We'll reach their camp in a few minutes. We'll only take the time to locate the horses, then get to work."

****

Jeb waved the men to a halt just outside the buffalo hunters' camp.

"Hoot, Nate, there's the horses, picketed off to the left," he whispered. "You ride in there, shoutin' and shootin', and panic those broncs. Create as big a ruckus as you can. Make sure you scatter 'em good. We don't want any of the men to catch one up and come after us. And be certain you don't use up all of your bullets scarin' the horses. You need to save some in case you've got to drill any man who tries to stop you. Soon as those horses are runnin' you head for home. We'll be right behind you, just as soon as we grab the water. And, one more time, be careful! You ready?"

Nate and Hoot nodded.

"How about you boys?"

Jim, Percy, and Carl also nodded their readiness. Jim and Percy took their six-guns from their holsters, while Carl pulled a wicked-looking, double-barreled shotgun from his saddle scabbard.

"This'll dang sure discourage any pursuit," he said.

"Good. Then let's go. Hoot, Nate…"

Hoot and Nate lifted their pistols from their holsters, walked their horses ahead for two hundred feet, then jabbed their spurs hard into their horses' ribs, with a yell. The startled mounts, even as tired as they were, leapt ahead in a dead run. Firing into the air, the two young Rangers galloped straight for the hunters' horses. The frightened animals jerked free of their picket line. Hoot and Nate rode straight into their midst, still shooting, slapping the laggards' rumps with their reins.

The terrified horses disappeared into the dark. Behind them, shouts and curses cut through the air, as the unsuspecting hunters realized their camp was being raided. Once their pistols were emptied, Hoot and Nate shoved them back in their holsters, lifted their rifles from their saddle boots, leaned over their horses' necks, and raced back toward the Ranger camp.

Angry shouts, then more shots rang out, as Jeb, Jim, Percy, and Carl rode into the hunters' camp, intent on getting the water the hunters had refused them, the water they so badly needed, or dying in the attempt.

"You reckon we should give 'em a hand, Hoot?" Nate asked.

"No. You heard what Jeb told us," Hoot answered. "Keep on ridin', as fast as Diablo's legs can carry you."

The shooting and yelling behind them continued as Hoot and Nate galloped away. A rifle shot, louder than the rest, split the air, followed by a man's yelp of pain.

"Sure hope that wasn't one of us," Nate said.

"I doubt it," Hoot answered. "We caught those hunters with their pants down. I don't imagine they even got off a shot. Don't fret none. Jeb and the rest of the boys will be right along."

****

Hoot's confidence the raid had gone off without a hitch was mistaken. While they had indeed been taken by surprise, several of the hunters, once over their initial shock, realized the running off of their horses was a diversion. They pulled out their guns and opened fire when Jeb, Percy, Jim, and Carl rode into their camp. Luckily for the four Rangers, the men had indeed been drinking heavily that night. Their eyes were still bleary, and their hasty response to the attack caused them to fire too quickly, without taking careful aim, then Ranger bullets downed two of them.

One of the remaining men took a snap shot at Jim Kelly's back. His bullet missed its target, but did clip Jim's left arm, then plowed a long furrow along Dooley, his strawberry roan's, neck. The impact knocked Jim forward in his saddle. Dooley whinnied in pain and fear when the bullet struck him, stumbled, and nearly went down. Jim grabbed the saddlehorn and somehow managed to hang on. Dooley regained his stride and kept running, with Jim slumped over his neck.

Carl's shotgun boomed when he pulled the trigger of one barrel, and three of the hunters were knocked off their feet by the spreading buckshot. Carl pulled his other trigger, and another man went down.

"That should hold 'em for a spell," he shouted. He shoved the shotgun back in its scabbard and pulled his pistol from its holster.

"Hurry and get those waterskins!" Jeb shouted. "There's still at least two of those hombres out there, and we don't know how badly the others have been hit. They're liable to start shootin' at us again any minute."

"I...I don't think...I can help...Jeb," Jim gasped. "I took a slug...through my...arm. Can't hardly...use it. Dooley got hit...too."

"How bad is it?" Jeb asked.

"Not sure. My arm's bleedin'...pretty heavy. Dooley took...the same bullet that hit...me...in his neck. He seems...to be holdin'...up. I think we'll both...make it back...to camp."

"We'll dang well make certain you do. Just get Dooley up here and we'll tie two of the skins to him," Jeb said.

"That, I can handle," Jim answered.

Jeb led the others to the wagons. They cut eight full waterskins loose, then tied them to their horses.

"Jim, you stick with me, where I can keep an eye on you," Jeb said, once the skins were secured, and everyone had remounted. "Now, let's get outta here."

They turned their horses to head for the safety of the Ranger camp.

****

Nate and Hoot had gone about a quarter mile when Hoot pulled Dusty down to a walk.

"What're you slowin' down for?" Nate asked.

"Blast it all, I can't listen to what Jeb ordered us to do; head back, no matter what," Hoot answered. "There was too much shootin' goin' on back there for me to rest easy. Leastwise until we find out what happened. We're gonna ride back and see if our pardners need any help. You with me?"

"Darn straight I am," Nate answered. "I was wonderin' how much farther we'd go before headin' back to lend a hand. Let's go."

They reversed direction and started back toward the hunters' camp. They had only gone a few hundred yards when they heard the hoof beats of hard-driven horses heading in their direction.

"Better hold up, until we see who's comin'," Hoot said. "Our pards, or those hunters."

He and Nate reined in, keeping their rifles at the ready. The oncoming horses drew nearer, the dust their hooves were throwing up now making a haze against the star-lit sky.

"They'll be on us any second, Nate. Be ready," Hoot warned. He lifted his rifle to his shoulder, and pointed it down the trail. Nate did the same.

"Here they come," Nate said, when the riders burst out of the scrub.

"Don't shoot," Hoot ordered, when he recognized Jeb's paint. "That's Jeb and the others. Dudley's spots give him away. Appears like one of the boys is hurt."

He waved his rifle in the air and shouted.

"Jeb! Over here. It's me'n Nate."

"Hoot! Hold on. We'll be right there," Jeb shouted back.

A moment later, they rode up to where Nate and Hoot waited.

"Thought I told you two to keep ridin', no matter what," Jeb grumbled. "Are you all right?"

"We're both fine," Hoot answered. "We couldn't keep goin', not without knowin' what happened to you fellers. Were you able to come up with any water? Are those hunters' gonna be on our trail?"

"Don't you see the skins hangin' from our saddles? Yeah, we got the water," Jeb answered. "As far as the hunters, mebbe, but I doubt it. We had to shoot 'em up pretty good. We got away clean, except for Jim. He took a slug through his arm. His horse got hit, too."

"How bad is it?" Nate asked.

"Bad enough," Jim answered. He was still slumped over, his left arm hanging limp. "I don't believe the bullet...clipped a bone, but it sure...tore me up. The arm's still bleedin' a lot. And Dooley's hurt...worse'n me."

"Mebbe we should patch you up before we head back," Hoot suggested.

"No time for that," Jim said. "We can't be certain...some of those hunters...won't be comin' after...us. I'll make it back...to camp, then we can work...on my arm. Jeb, let's keep movin'."

"Right, Jim."

The six men put their horses into a lope, not wanting to push the exhausted animals any harder. A short while later, they rode into camp.

"Up and at 'em!" Jeb shouted. "We've got water, boys. Water for everyone!"

As Jeb expected, both Captain Quincy and Lieutenant Bob were already awake, and waiting for them.

"And just where did you get that water, Ranger Rollins?" Quincy asked.

"Funny thing. We went out lookin' for some, and found all these full skins of it, just lyin' alongside the trail. It must've fallen off someone's wagons. Or mebbe outta heaven."

"Yeah. Mebbe some angel dropped it," Hoot said.

"And what about those jugs I see tied to Carl's saddle?" Quincy pressed.

"I liberated them from some poor soul we stumbled across," Carl answered. "He said he'd found religion, and tried to swear off the evils of spirits, but just couldn't seem to quit. So I gave him a hand. Helped him stop sinnin', and drinkin' to excess."

"I see."

All of the men, except the wounded George and Dan, were gathering around the captain. "Tom, Larry, Dakota. Help get those waterskins off these horses, then get some buckets, fill 'em, and start waterin' our animals," he ordered. "Tell Phil to bring in the remuda, so they can have a drink. Ken, you and Joe get some water to George and Dan. Take some for yourselves, then get back to your posts, until your watch is up. Jeb, I don't suppose anyone would be followin' you, lookin' for this water, would they?"

"I doubt it, Cap'n. Although I suppose it is possible. You know there are all sorts of outlaws on the prowl in these parts. But we didn't see any."

"Then how'd Jim get shot?"

Jim was still hunched over in the saddle, supporting his left arm with his right hand.

"Dropped my rifle...and plugged...myself, Cap'n Dave," Jim said. "Shot poor...Dooley, too. I sure hope Phil can...patch him up."

"Of course you did," Quincy replied, wryly. "Well, get down off your horse, and take care of that wound. Then, all of you get some water. Carl, I don't suppose that scattergun you're holdin's been fired?"

"Purely by accident," Carl said.

"Naturally," Quincy said. "By accident, twice. Both barrels. And of course, no one else's weapons have been fired, either. And also, of course, not one of those bullets that 'weren't fired' hit a blamed thing."

"We can't say as to that," Jeb answered. "It was pitch dark out there."

"Even you didn't see a thing, Percy?" Quincy asked. "You, with eyes sharp as a cat's in the night?"

"As Jeb says, it was awful dark, Cap'n."

"Very well. However, as soon as Jim's arm is cared for, and y'all get some water, I want to see all of you."

"Yessir, Cap'n," Jeb said. "C'mon, men, let's get that water."

"I'd like Jeb'n Nate to give me a hand bandagin' up my arm, Cap'n," Jim said. "It'd be a bit of trouble for me to try'n do it one-handed."

"All right. Jeb, Nate, you go with him."

"Sure," Jeb said. "C'mon, Jim, let's get you patched up."

Jim, with Jeb and Hoot following, rode Dooley over to the chuck wagon, where most of what remained of his medical supplies were kept, and slid off his horse. He slumped against Dooley's side, then slipped to the ground.

"Reckon I must've bled...more'n I thought," he said. "I'm feelin'...kinda weak."

"We'll take care of you, Jim," Jeb assured him, as he and Nate dismounted. "Nate, you know where Jim's supplies are. Get 'em."

"Right away."

Nate climbed into the wagon to get the medical supplies. By the time he got them, Jeb had propped Jim against one of the wagon wheels, and had slid off his shirt. The buffalo hunter's shot had punched its way through Jim's left arm, halfway between elbow and shoulder, leaving two holes, one where it had entered, and a larger one where it exited.

"Jim, you're dang lucky that hunter's aim was off, probably from him bein' fool drunk," Jeb said. "From the size of that wound, he was usin' a Sharps .50. If that slug had hit your arm dead center, it would've torn it clean off. Or, if he'd got you in the back..."

"Tell me later...how lucky...I am, Jeb," Jim said, with a soft laugh. He looked at his wounded arm, then cursed softly.

"You're gonna have...to pack this arm...to stop the bleedin'," he said. "Jeb, get my...tobacco pouch outta my...vest pocket. Nate, take the bottle of...whiskey and...some bandages...outta my kit."

"Right away," Jeb answered.

The requested items were procured.

"You've got 'em?" Jim said. "Good. "Nate, pour some of the...whiskey into the holes...in my arm. Douse 'em good."

"All right." Nate poured a liberal amount of the liquor over the wounds. Jim bit down hard, gritting his teeth against the stinging pain.

"You doin' okay, Jim?" Nate asked.

"I'm all right," Jim answered. "Jeb, sprinkle tobacco...into those...holes," he ordered. "Nate, that helps stop bleedin', and also keeps...wounds from festerin', in case you're...wonderin'. Jeb, make sure it packs...tight, you hear me?"

"Just like packin' your old pipe," Jeb said. He poured most of the contents of the pouch into the bullet holes.

"Best I can do," he said, once he was finished.

"That'll be fine," Jim said. "Nate, pour some more...whiskey over the...holes. After that, take...one of the bandages, douse it...with more whiskey, then tie it around...my arm. Once that's done, Jeb'll make...a sling with my...bandanna, and I'll be good as new. And where...in blue blazes...is Phil? Dooley needs...doctorin'."

"I'm right here, Jim," Phil said, as he rode up and dismounted. "I'll take care of your horse. You just worry about yourself."

"Okay, I'll try, but I'm awful worried about ol' Dooley," Jim said. After Phil led Dooley away, Jeb and Nate finished working on Jim.

"All we can do for now, Jim," Jeb said. "I reckon you'd better just stay here and rest. Be right back with some water. We'll square things with the cap'n for you."

"No. I'm comin' with...you," Jim insisted. "Just help...me up."

"Are you sure?" Jeb asked.

"I'm positive."

"All right. Nate..."

"Sure."

Jim was helped to his feet, then, with Jeb and Nate supporting him, went with them to see Captain Quincy. The other members of the raiding party were already with him. Phil was also there.

"Got some water for you three," Percy said. He passed tin mugs filled to the brim to Jeb, Nate, and Jim, who took them, and eagerly downed the contents.

"Jim, I've gotta get back to your horse," Phil said. "I just wanted to let you know Dooley should be all right. The bullet tore a pretty good path along his neck, but that's all. He was lucky. It didn't sever his spinal column, or hit him in the head and bury itself in his brain." He paused, then winked knowingly at Jim. "Next time, be more careful with your rifle, will ya?"

"I sure will be," Jim answered.

"Phil, get on outta here," Captain Quincy ordered. "I want to speak with these men, in private."

"All right, Cap'n."

Quincy waited until Phil was out of earshot before speaking.

"Gentlemen," he began. "First, I want to thank you for most likely saving the lives of every man in this company. Your efforts are appreciated."

"Thanks, Cap'n," Jeb said.

"I'm not finished," Quincy replied. "Having said that, I'm a bit suspicious about where you came up with that water. No, I'm positive I know where you came up with that water. Officially, I'm supposed to say your methods were wrong, and you should be disciplined. Officially, that is. Unofficially, excellent job. Now, as far as any discipline, I figure listenin' to my little speech just now was punishment enough. So get outta my sight, get some more water, and get some rest. We'll start again for Fort Stockton at sunup. But before you go, I've got one of the jugs that Carl...ahem...'liberated'. Y'all might as well take a slug from it."

"Why, thank you kindly, Cap'n Dave," Jeb said.

The jug was passed around, every man taking a swallow. Hoot flushed after having his drink. "Smooth. Real smooth," he said, then broke into a fit of coughing. He passed the jug to Nate.

"Your turn, pardner."

Nate lifted the jug to his lips, took a sip, then a good-sized gulp of the fiery liquor.

"You're right, Hoot. Smooth as silk," he said, gasping. He passed the jug back to Captain Quincy.

"I think everyone's had enough for tonight," Quincy said. "Go on, get outta here."

"Yes, sir! Cap'n!" Jeb answered. "You heard him, men. Let's go."

****

"Hoot, I want to check on Red before I turn in," Nate said, as they headed for their bedrolls.

"Of course you do," Hoot said. "I want to check on Dusty one last time, too."

"Hoot," Nate continued. "Cap'n Dave knew all along what we were up to, didn't he?"

"Of course he did, ya idjit," Hoot answered. He smacked Nate playfully on the arm. "He knew some of us would go back for that water. No one treats the Rangers like those buffalo hunters did and gets away with it. The only thing he didn't know was who'd go after 'em. Now, let's take care of our broncs, then get some shut-eye."

3

Two days later, around mid-afternoon, they reached the outskirts of Saint Gall. The bustling community had sprung up around the Army's Fort Stockton, and indeed many people, including the Texas Rangers, mistakenly referred to the town itself by that name.

One reason the town's site had been chosen for a settlement was its proximity to Comanche Springs, one of the few large sources of dependable water in the area. The original settlers were mainly Irish, German, and Mexican immigrants from San Antonio. It served as a hub for the region, catering to ranchers, farmers, freighters, and buffalo hunters.*

"We'll set up camp here," Captain Quincy said. They had stopped alongside a stream which emanated from the springs. "Soon as we're finished, you'll all have permission to go into town. Not everyone at once, of course. I'll draw names, which will set the order."

"How long do you figure on stayin' in town, Cap'n?" Lieutenant Bob asked.

"I'm not certain," Quincy answered. "Probably two nights, mebbe three. I have to send a telegram to Headquarters to let them know we've arrived, and ask what our next orders will be. And tell them the gang which was raisin' so much ruckus, includin' murderin' Nate's family and killin' so many of our pards, is finished. That means we have to wait for a reply, which might take a day. We have to resupply, of course. We also need to have permanent repairs made to the chuck wagon. In addition, I want to try and pick up a few new recruits. And I'd like to get George and Dan to a proper doctor, so he can examine them. Jim, too."

"There's no need for that, Cap'n," Dan objected. "I'm doin' just fine."

"Me, too," Jim added.

"The same goes for me," George said. "I'll be back on my feet and cookin' for you boys again in no time."

"Nonetheless, humor me," Quincy answered. "Bob, I'll need you to notify the town marshal we're in town, and will be here for a few days. I'll ride into town with you. I'd also like to notify the commander at Fort Stockton of our presence, and possibly to arrange a meeting with him."

"Sure, Dave," Lieutenant Bob answered.

"Good. Men, let's set up camp," Quincy ordered. "The faster that's done, the faster y'all will get to town."

****

Unlike the impression most Easterners had from reading dime novel stories about the West, the first thing most cowboys did when they reached town *wasn't* to head straight for the saloons, gambling parlors, and dance halls. After weeks or months on the trail, the first thing they wanted to do was clean up. Drinking and gambling could wait a bit.

So, the first two stops most cowboys made were to the local Chinese laundry, or washerwoman's, to drop off their trail-filthy clothes to be cleaned, then on to the local barbers or hotels, for shaves, trims, and baths. The Rangers, Nate and Hoot included, were no exceptions. The two young lawmen dropped off most of their clothes at a laundry run by a local widow, then went to the barber shop located inside the Fort Stockton Hotel.

"Do you want a haircut *and* shave?" the barber asked Nate, once he was settled in the chair.

"Well, yeah, I guess so," Nate said, somewhat taken aback. He knew he'd grown a thin beard over the past few weeks, but he hadn't realized it was that noticeable.

"Mister, you'd have to find some whiskers first," Hoot said, with a laugh.

"At least I don't have to wear a beard to cover up an ugly mug like yours," Nate shot back. "Mister, go ahead and give me that shave. If my pardner wants one, don't do it. Horses get spooked, ladies faint dead away, dogs howl, and little kids run off if he steps out on the street without whiskers coverin' up his face."

"Fine. I'll lather you right up."

Never having been shaved before, Nate relished the soothing feel of the hot lather against his sun-toughened skin, the smooth glide of the razor over his face and neck. In a short while, he was shaved, his hair neatly trimmed. Once Hoot's barbering was also completed, they asked about arranging for baths.

"Those are taken care of by the hotel," the barber explained. "They have bathing rooms in an addition out back. There's even a separate one for the ladies." He shook his head. "What's this world coming to, public baths for females? It's shocking. Next thing you know, even decent women will be showing their ankles in public. Now, a lotta folks around here say we're just bein' up to date, keepin' up with the times, but mark my words, nothin' good's gonna come of it. Well, it's out of my hands. Two bits for your shaves and haircuts. If you want those baths, stop at the front desk."

"We will, mister, and much obliged," Hoot said. A few minutes later, he and Nate were relaxing in zinc tubs filled with hot, soapy water.

"Hoot, I never thought a bath would feel this good," Nate said, as he settled more deeply into his tub. "I'll be ten pounds lighter once I get all the trail dirt scrubbed offa me."

"Boy howdy, you've got that right," Hoot agreed. "I can feel this hot water just meltin' the aches outta my muscles. I could stay in this tub for weeks."

"You'd look like a dried up ol' prune if you did," Nate answered, laughing. "I just thought of this. What if a couple of women made a mistake, and came in here instead of the ladies' bathin' room. Wouldn't that be somethin'?"

"It sure would," Hoot answered. "And I can tell you one thing for certain. If any women did come in here by accident, they'd just naturally head for me."

"I don't hardly think so," Nate retorted. "I'm better lookin' than you are, by a long shot. You wouldn't stand a chance. Those females would come straight for me."

"Nuh-uh." Hoot shook his head. "I'm bigger'n you are, and filled out more. Women don't want a skinny feller like you. If any women wandered in here, they'd take one look at my chest, and my big shoulders, and practically fall into the tub with me."

"Yeah, 'cause they'd faint dead away soon as they caught sight of your ugly face, pardner," Nate said. He sighed. "I reckon we don't have to worry about that anyway. Ain't no women ever gonna come in here."

"And with our luck, even if some did, they'd be fat, and uglier'n a mule's butt," Hoot answered. He snapped his fingers. "Wait a minute! I just had an idea. How about *we* go to *them*?"

"What d'ya mean, Hoot? We can't just sashay in on a bunch of women takin' their baths," Nate said. "They'd scream and holler, and raise one heckuva fuss. We'd get in trouble, for certain."

"No we wouldn't," Hoot insisted. "We just go in there like we took a wrong turn, and pretend we made a mistake, that's all. C'mon, think about it. This could finally be our chance to see a woman without her clothes on."

"Hoot, it won't work," Nate objected. "How're we gonna walk over there, buck naked like we are? Someone'd be sure and spot us."

"I didn't mean buck naked, ya idjit," Hoot said. "We'd get dressed first. Then we'd head over there, carryin' our towels like we was just comin' to take a bath, and got into the wrong room. We don't want to scare folks, which'd sure happen if they saw you in your birthday suit."

He threw a wet washcloth at Nate, hitting him in the face. Nate splashed a handful of water at him. Hoot splashed one back, and they quickly became engaged in a full-fledged water fight. Finally, both fell back, laughing.

"Well, it was a thought, anyway," Nate said. "An interestin' one, but just a thought. How much time you reckon we got left to soak?"

"I'd say about fifteen minutes or so," Hoot said. "Don't forget, we paid an extra two bits for some more time in these here tubs."

"And worth every penny." Nate picked up his washcloth and began scrubbing under his right arm. The door burst open, and two heavily rouged and powdered women, one blonde, the other a redhead, walked into the room.

"There you boys are," the redhead shouted. "Sorry we're late. We've just been achin' to meet you."

"What?" Hoot yelped, and slid under the water, as the blonde headed straight for him.

Nate didn't have the chance to react before the redhead sat on the edge of his tub, and put a hand on his shoulder.

"Ida Mae, this one's as cute as a button," she said. "What happened to yours?"

"He seems a bit shy, Betty Lou," Ida Mae answered. "But he can't stay under forever. He'll be surfacin' any minute now."

"What...what are you ladies doin' here?" Nate

stammered.

"Why, we came to see you, sugar plum," Betty Lou answered.

"But, but..."

"Here's mine," Ida Mae said, when Hoot surfaced, spluttering. Before he could disappear under the suds again, she grabbed his arm.

"Oh, no, you don't, honey child. You're not gettin' away from me again."

"There must be some mistake," Nate said. "Hoot—"

"I-I can't help you, pardner," Hoot said, his voice almost a squeak. "This here female's got me cornered."

"There ain't no mistake. We came to see you boys," Betty Lou said. She ran her hand over Nate's chest.

"We sure did," Ida Mae confirmed. She pulled Hoot half out of the tub, then began to rub his belly.

"But, but, we wasn't lookin' for no ladies," Hoot said. "We was just wantin' to get cleaned up."

"Well, we can sure help you do that," Ida Mae said. She picked up a washcloth and began to scrub Hoot's back.

"I don't need any help," Hoot half-shouted. "We was just about done, anyway."

"You hear that, Ida Mae?" Betty Lou asked. "They're just about finished washin'. I reckon that means they want our help dryin' off." She picked up a towel and looked at Nate. "Whenever you're ready, sugar."

Nate's face was flushed beet red, and it wasn't from the hot water.

"I...I can't get outta this tub. Not in front of you ladies. It ain't decent. Please, just leave us alone."

"Are you sure that's what you want?" Betty Lou asked.

"Yeah, yeah. That goes for me, too," Hoot said.

"Well, we certainly don't stay anyplace we're not wanted," Ida Mae pouted. "C'mon, Betty. Let's go find us some fellers who'll appreciate us."

"There are plenty of those in this town," Betty Lou said. "We don't need to waste our time here. Good-bye, boys." She picked up some suds with the tip of her finger, then ran it down Nate's nose. "That's so you don't forget me."

She and Ida Mae flounced out of the room, leaving Nate and Hoot staring after them.

"What the devil was that all about?" Nate asked.

"I dunno, Nate, but you sure didn't know which way to turn when those females busted in on us," Hoot answered.

"Me? You're the one who nearly drowned himself, hidin' under the water from that blonde," Nate retorted.

"Yeah, I guess I did," Hoot answered. "But I came back up, didn't I?"

"Probably only because your lungs were gonna burst," Nate said. "If you had gills, you'd still be under water. At least I let mine touch my chest."

"Yeah, mebbe. But I got my belly rubbed," Hoot shot back. He smiled at the thought.

"So what?" Nate answered. "Let's face it, pard. Neither one of us knew what to do with those women. I reckon we'll never get us a girl."

The door swung open again. This time, Jeb, Dakota, and Lieutenant Bob walked into the room. They looked around.

"Seems like they're already gone, boys," Bob said.

"Seems like," Dakota agreed.

"What're all of you doin', bustin' in on us like this?" Hoot demanded.

"Us? We came to see some friends we sent you," Jeb answered. "But I don't see 'em anywhere around here. You two didn't chase 'em off, did you?"

"You mean those women? Of course we didn't," Hoot said. "Ain't that right, Nate?"

"'Course we didn't chase 'em off," Nate said.

"Then where are they?" Dakota asked.

"They just left, that's all," Hoot answered.

"Boys, you don't reckon ol' Hoot and Nate, here, were frightened by those females, do you?" Bob asked.

"Nate and Hoot, two rough, tough, fightin' Texas Rangers?" Jeb said. "Not hardly. I figure they were too much for those women to handle."

"That's gotta be it," Dakota said. "The ladies knew they were in over their heads, so they left."

"I'd say the only one in over his head was Hoot," Jeb answered, with a glance at Hoot's wet hair, which was plastered to his scalp. "Well, it don't matter. Those gals are gone, and they ain't comin' back. Let's go get us some whiskey."

He burst into laughter, joined by Dakota and Bob, as they left Hoot and Nate to their misery.

"I think I'm just gonna curl up and die, right in this here tub," Nate said.

"That makes the both of us," Hoot said. The door swung open again.

"Oh, no. Now what?" Nate groaned.

"It's only me," the bath attendant said. "I just need to remind you boys your time is up. There are other customers waiting, so you have to clear out, right now. Get dressed and get movin'."

"We'll be done in five minutes," Hoot said

"See that you are." The attendant slammed the door as he left.

"I reckon we'll just have to shoot ourselves, Hoot," Nate said.

"I reckon so," Hoot agreed. He shook his head. "I reckon so."

****

"Well, Hoot, since we really don't want to shoot ourselves, what do you want to do now?" Nate asked, after they left the hotel and stood in front of it, looking up and down Main Street.

"I figure one of two things. Either we can get supper, or we can try gettin' drunk again...or both," Hoot answered.

"You don't want to try'n find some women? Mebbe with some different ones we'll have better luck," Nate said.

"And get ourselves shot outta the saddle again, Nate? Nah. I reckon those women can wait until the next town we hit," Hoot said. "Now, let's decide. Are you more thirsty, or hungry?"

"After all those days without water, I'm definitely more thirsty," Nate said. "We can always eat later."

"Good. My thinkin' exactly. We'll head for the nearest saloon."

They started down the street, but only got about a block before they noticed a large crowd, standing in front of the Cavalrymen's Saloon. Its members were murmuring with anticipation.

"Looks like somethin's goin' on there, Nate," Hoot said. "I reckon we might as well find out what."

He and Nate quickened their pace, reaching the crowd a minute later. Hoot nudged a man at its edge.

"Howdy, mister. You mind tellin' us what's goin' on?"

"Howdy yourself, son. We're waitin' for a fight to break out in there, anytime now."

"Why?" Hoot asked.

"Well, you see, this here saloon is a soldier's bar," the man answered. "It caters to the buffalo soldiers. A few of 'em were standin' out front when some Rangers came along. Dunno what happened for certain, but it seems one of the Rangers fell flat on his face in the road. He yelled he was shoved by one of the soldiers. They laughed, and went on inside. Next thing anyone knew, the Rangers followed 'em right on in. There's been a lot of hollerin' goin' on, and we figure fists are gonna start flyin' any minute now."

"Nate, we'd better get in there, and give our pardners a hand," Hoot said. "Let's go."

"I'm right with you, Hoot," Nate said, then raised his voice to be heard above the crowd. "Let us through. We're Rangers."

The two young lawmen elbowed their way through the crowd, then pushed through the batwing doors. On the right side of the saloon was a group of eight soldiers from Fort Stockton. Nate recognized one of them as the burly sergeant from Captain Anders's patrol, Travis Burnham. On the left were Rangers Ken Demarest, Tom Tomlinson, Dakota Stevens, Lieutenant Bob Berkeley, Jeb Rollins, and Carl Swan. And in the center of the room, holding a sawed off shotgun, stood the bartender. The twin barrels of that Greener swung from side to side, first pinning the soldiers, then the Rangers, then back. Adding to its menace was the appearance of the bartender himself, a tall, broad-shouldered black man, with a shaved head, who stood scowling at both groups.

"I warned y'all once, and I ain't gonna warn you again, I won't tolerate any fightin' in my place," he rumbled, in a deep voice. "Y'all just settle whatever problems you have peaceable-like, then be on your way. Anyone who starts somethin' will find himself cut in two by the horseshoe nails and rock salt I keep this ol' scattergun loaded with."

"I ain't leavin' until I take care of the big galoot who pushed me," Carl said.

"And I've already told you, you chucklehead, I didn't push you," Burnham retorted. "You done tripped over those big clodhoppers you have for feet."

"Why you..." Carl started to rush Burnham, only to stop short when the bartender swung his shotgun and leveled it at his belly.

"Just hold it right there, mister," he said. "Same for you, Travis. Now, y'all are gonna listen to me. Ranger, you claim Travis pushed you. Travis, you say he fell, all by hisself. Seems to me ain't neither of you's gonna admit the other is wrong. So, that leaves us two choices. Either the whole lot of you can beat each other's brains out, or mebbe even pull out your guns and get yourselves killed over nothin' but foolishness, or you can handle this sensible like. Now, I can already see none of you are gonna walk away until this is settled, so I've got a proposal to make. I'm givin' y'all a choice, actually. All of you can just walk outta here, which I know won't happen, or the two men who started all this in the first place can settle it, man to man...by arm wrestlin'. That way no one gets hurt, and trouble gets stopped before it starts. Ranger, Travis, you both agreeable?"

"I dunno, Patry," Burnham answered.

The bartender turned to pin Burnham with his shotgun.

"I said, are you agreeable, Travis?"

The burly sergeant hesitated for just a moment, swallowed hard, and then said, quietly, "I reckon I am."

"Good. How about you, Ranger?"

"I guess I am, too," Carl said.

"A wise decision," the bartender stated. "Now, since you Rangers don't know me, my name's Horace Patry, and I own this place. A couple of you boys move a table and two chairs to the center of the room. And don't do anythin' foolish."

"Jeb, get a table," Lieutenant Bob ordered.

"Macy, get two chairs," Burnham told one of his men.

"We might as well make this a bit more interestin', and have a little wagerin'," Patry said. "One of you tell the folks outside they can join us, and place bets on the outcome of the match, if they're so inclined. Better make it one of you Rangers. They'll be more likely to accept the invite from a white man, rather than a black fella."

"I'll do it," Ken said. He stepped outside, and extended

Patry's invitation. The men in the crowd, enticed by the opportunity to perhaps make some easy money, overcame their reluctance to enter a blacks' only establishment and hurried inside. Carl and Burnham took their seats at the table, while their partners, and the crowd, gathered around them.

"Gentlemen," Patry said, "I'm gonna establish the rules, before we get started. There will be a ten-minute period to place wagers. I'll hold all bets, and will take ten percent of the wagers as the house's cut. I'll also be the referee, and my rulings will be final. To win, a man will have to take two out of three matches. Are there any questions before we begin? Good. Start placing your bets."

For the next ten minutes, money was passed, the bets being about even between the burly cavalry sergeant and the smaller, but huskier, Ranger. Once all bets were placed, Patry called for quiet. Carl and Burnham took their seats, rolled up their right shirtsleeves, and grasped each other's right fist, elbows on the table. They glared at each other.

"Gentlemen, all bets are placed. Are you ready?"

"I am," Burnham said. Carl nodded.

"Good. Go!"

Burnham snapped Carl's arm back, slamming it to the table. Carl's fellow Rangers, and the spectators who had bet on him, groaned, while the rest of the soldiers, and those who had bet on Burnham, cheered.

"This is gonna be easier than I figured," Burnham said, grinning. "Why don't you just make it easy on yourself and quit right now, Ranger?"

"You ain't gonna take me that easy," Carl retorted. "You caught me before I was set, that's all."

"Are you both ready to go again?" Patry asked.

Both men nodded, and set themselves.

"Go!"

This time, Carl took the edge, gradually forcing Burnham's forearm toward the table. Then, Burnham recovered, pushing back, until once again both men's arms were perpendicular to the table. Sweat broke out on the two men's foreheads, and their muscles bulged as they struggled for an advantage. Finally, Carl got the leverage he needed. Imperceptibly at first, he pushed Burnham's arm back, then the momentum increased, and he forced Burnham's arm flat.

"The Ranger takes this match," Patry announced. "We'll take a ten minute break, so the contestants can have a beer, and those of you so inclined might purchase a drink."

Patry gave each of the contestants a foamy mugful of beer. Nate and Hoot joined the men bellied up to the bar, and ordered beers for themselves. Ten minutes passed, then once again Carl and Burnham were set.

"Go!"

Both men strained, neither able to budge the other. They grunted and groaned with the effort, struggling to gain the slightest advantage. The veins on Carl's arm stood out like cords, Burnham's brow furrowed as he fought his adversary. When he attempted to heave Carl's arm over, the muscles in his back bulged, ripping his shirt down the middle. For five minutes, their arms wavered back and forth but little, while the spectators cheered them on. Then, slowly, but inevitably, Burnham forced Carl's arm back. With one final push, he shoved it to the table.

"Travis Burnham is our winner!" Patry announced.

"Congratulations, Sergeant," Carl said. "You beat me, fair and square."

"Thanks. Good fight, Ranger. I wouldn't want to have to take you on again," Burnham answered. "Buy you a beer?"

"I wouldn't mind that," Carl said.

"Good. Horace, two beers," Burnham called to the bartender.

"Comin' right up, soon's I pass out the winnin's," Patry answered.

Both men sat, rubbing their wrists, while they waited for the drinks.

"I reckon I owe you an apology," Carl said. "Thinkin' on it, I must've tripped on my own, like you said."

"No apology needed," Burnham answered. "You stumbled, but I helped you the rest of the way down. We gonna have to fight again?"

"I don't think so." Carl shook his head. "I'd rather just sit here and down a few more beers, if it's all the same to you."

"That sounds like a fine idea to me," Burnham said.

Over at the bar, Nate and Hoot had joined the other Rangers. They had each ordered a second beer.

"Fellers," Jeb said. "I hope there ain't any hard feelin's over us sendin' those ladies into your baths. It was just a little joke. We didn't expect anythin' more'n what happened to happen."

"Yeah, we was just having some fun with you," Dakota added. "We sure didn't expect you to take up with those gals or anythin', less'n you wanted to."

"No, there's no hard feelin's," Hoot answered. "Those gals weren't our type, anyway. Were they, Nate?"

"No, they sure weren't," Nate answered. "Not hardly at all."

"Then that's settled," Jeb said. "Tell you what. I'll buy you both another beer."

"That sounds good to me," Nate said.

For the next two hours, Nate, Hoot, and their companions stayed in the Cavalrymen's, drinking beer and trading war stories with the soldiers. Shortly before midnight, they headed back to camp, Nate and Hoot feeling a little woozy, but nowhere near as bad as they had the night back in San Saba. Once they ducked into their tent and crawled into their bunks, they were quickly asleep.

****

Two days later, Captain Quincy assembled the company, in front of his tent.

"Men," he said. "I have several pieces of business to discuss with you today. First, I'd like you to meet the seven men I have recruited into our ranks: Shirley Bruneau, who goes by Shad, Montana Davis, Diego Sandoval, Frank Washington, his son Pete, Stan Zubrowski, and Morey Carson. This actually brings us up to twenty-two men, so we have a full complement, plus a couple of extras. Let's give them a big Ranger welcome."

The gathered Rangers cheered and applauded their new partners.

"Good," Quincy said. "For you new men, you'll be ridin' with some of the finest hombres ever to work for the outfit. I'm certain y'all will make Rangers every bit as good as they are. Now, for all of you, we have received our orders from Headquarters. We've been assigned to patrol the Rio Grande, all along the Big Bend, from Presidio to the Pecos River, for at least the next three months. Unfortunately, for those of you with families, that means we won't be returning to Austin until sometime next year. You won't be home for the holidays. So, if any of you want to resign your commission, speak up right now. I'll let you out of your enlistment, honorably, with no hard feelin's and no questions asked. I'd rather you do that instead of mebbe decidin' you've had enough of days on end in the saddle, bad food, sleepin' on the hard ground, and gettin' shot at all the time, a couple of months down the road, and desert the company. I know I ain't lookin' forward to not seein' my wife and kids for who knows how long. So if any of you want out, say so."

He was met with silence, and a shaking of heads.

85

"I reckon everyone wants to stick with the outfit, Cap'n Dave," Lieutenant Bob said.

"That's right, Cap'n," Ken added. "I miss my family too, but what we're doin' is awful important. Me, and the rest of the boys, will see it through."

"Fine. I really appreciate that, all of you," Quincy said. "So, we'll move out, first thing in the mornin'. I just have one more thing to say. I'm especially grateful for the way you handled yourselves during our stay in Fort Stockton. Major Bliss sends his compliments, as does Marshal Wolf. They received no complaints at all about your conduct in town. The major did have some doubts for a spell, however.

"It seems several buffalo hunters made a complaint to him, claiming some men who matched the descriptions of a few of you jumped them, killed four of their number and wounded several more, then stole their water supply.

"I was able to convince him none of you had anything to do with that attack, and that, in fact, we had received word of those men making the complaint possibly being the same ones who were suspected of stealing hides and poisoning water holes.

"That means we leave here on good terms with the Army, and with the citizens of Fort Stockton—I mean, Saint Gall. I'm proud of each and every one of you. Now, take care of your horses, check over your gear, and get ready to travel."

4

After leaving Fort Stockton, the Rangers faced nearly two hundred miles of travel through some of the most isolated, rugged territory in the state of Texas, until they reached their destination, deep in the Big Bend, hard by the Rio Grande and the Mexican border. There were no other settlements in the area they would cross. The only signs of civilization they might possibly come across for the next few weeks, or even months, would be a few scattered ranches, or perhaps an isolated trading post. However, this vast wilderness, unoccupied except for those lonely outposts, was an ideal place for men on the run from the law to hide. Renegades of all stripes—whites, Mexicans, or Indians—could raid with impunity, then disappear into the myriad canyons and badlands of this lawless territory. Even a group of lawmen as determined as the Texas Rangers were to bring the law to this lawless region as often as not lost their quarry...or their lives, to bushwhack bullets.

Making their lives even more difficult was the unforgiving land itself. The temperature could soar well into the nineties during the day, then plunge into the forties once the sun went down. Sudden, violent thunderstorms could drench the men, the storms' wind-driven rain soaking them, even under their wide-brimmed hats, and through their slickers. The rain would mix with the dust driven before the storm, making it seem as if it were raining mud. The downpours turned the earth into more mud, the trails into quagmires, and filled normally dry washes rim to rim with roiling flood waters, which could easily drown a man and his horse. However, those storms were infrequent, and most of their rains quickly ran off, or soaked into the thirsty ground, dried up before they could provide any relief. Throughout this parched, arid, sunbaked region, water was scarce, and game even more so. In what few waterholes there were, the water was more often than not unfit to drink, polluted with alkali, bitter and unpalatable, poisonous to man and beast. The food and water which George carried in his chuck wagon would have to be carefully rationed. Under such difficult conditions, nerves grew taut, and tempers short. Even the slightest remark, made in jest, could rub a man the wrong way, and his anger would flare. It took all the leadership skills Captain Quincy had to keep arguments among the men from breaking into full-blown fistfights, or worse.

Nate was now toughened nearly as much as any of the other men. He rode without complaining, except for the general grousing about the dust and the heat, as did the rest of the men. He drank very sparingly, and was able to get along just fine for the day with a few strips of jerky and some hardtack for his meals, washed down with a few swallows of tepid water from his canteen. Unfortunately, even he was not immune from the short tempers affecting all of the men. A slight misstep would get him into some serious trouble.

Despite the hardships, once they reached the Big Bend, the next several weeks seemed to pass quickly, at least to Nate. It took the Rangers ten days to make the Rio Grande. Once they arrived, their time was taken up by searching for smugglers, cattle rustlers, horse thieves, bank robbers, killers, and other assorted desperadoes who plagued Texas and its citizens.

The Lone Star State's vast expanses attracted scores of outlaws, who took advantage of its rugged vastness and miles of empty territory to commit their crimes, then disappear from the law. With local authority non-existent, it fell to the Texas Rangers to track down those men. And the Big Bend was one of the most rugged sections of all, with its canyons and draws, its forbidding mountains, its harsh deserts.

This was the harshest land Texas contained, with searing deserts, deep canyons, and soaring mountains. Its climate was just as harsh, with temperatures that could climb to one hundred degrees or more in summer, yet plunge far below freezing in winter. The variety of vegetation was astounding, including everything from desert dwelling cactus and yucca, to tough grasses, to, at the higher elevations, pines and Douglas firs usually found much farther north.

The animals inhabiting the territory were just as varied, with everything from heat-loving rodents and snakes, to deer, mountain lions, and Mexican wolves.

In addition, its proximity to Mexico made it even more attractive to those seeking to escape the reach of Texas justice. Just a short swim across the Rio Grande brought a man into Mexico, where he was shielded from Texas law and lawmen...or so he thought. Many an outlaw who believed himself safe in Mexico found out, to his dismay, the Texas Rangers quite often didn't let a little thing like an international boundary keep them from following their quarry across the Rio, to be brought back to the Lone Star State and face the consequences of his crimes. Or, if he resisted, to die from Ranger bullets, in a foreign land.

Captain Quincy set up camp in Blue Creek Canyon, about a quarter mile upstream from where the creek emptied into the Rio Grande. The location, along the banks of Blue Creek, provided a source of steady water, and decent grazing for the horses and mules, hard to find in this arid region. Some good-sized cottonwoods, junipers, pin oaks, and bigtooth maples offered shade. Quincy didn't wish to camp along the Rio Grande itself, since the river could flood with little warning, possibly washing away the camp and endangering lives.

In addition, he didn't want any prying eyes from the Mexican side of the river to be able to keep watch on the Rangers' camp. The remote location was about sixty miles southeast of Presidio, the nearest settlement. When supplies were needed, it would be a four-day round trip to town. However, the Rangers were almost entirely self-sufficient, used to living off the land, so any such trips would be few and far between.

Once the camp was established, Quincy divided his company into three patrols, which would cover the hundreds of square miles to which they'd been assigned. Jeb Rollins was promoted to Sergeant, and placed in charge of one patrol, to which Nate was assigned. The others in Jeb's patrol were Hoot, Tom, Carl, Dakota, along with two of the new men, Stan Zubrowski and Morey Carson, who both had been deputy marshals in Saint Gall.

Even though Nate had grown in stature, both physically and as a Ranger, he was still the most inexperienced lawman in the group. Nonetheless, as he'd done during the search for the gang which had killed his family, he proved more than capable in helping track down and round up many of the outlaws plaguing west Texas.

Summer had faded into autumn, September into late October. Jeb's patrol had several brushes with outlaw bands, most of which ended in gunplay. Luckily, while they had killed a number of renegades, and chased many more back into Mexico, none of the men had been gunned down, nor even seriously wounded. The only injuries suffered were by Tom, who was grazed along his ribs by a rustler's bullet, and Morey, who took a bad spill when his horse stumbled and fell.

With it being mid-autumn, the weather was gradually turning cooler. In the labyrinth of canyons, mountains, and badlands which was the Big Bend, even the most experienced frontiersman could lose his way. That was exactly what happened to Jeb and his men. They had spent three days trying to find their way out of a maze of winding canyons, which seemed to twist back into each other. They finally emerged into a relatively open area, a broad, shallow arroyo. However, to make matters worse, the wind was increasing. In fitful gusts, it picked up sand and dust, lifting them high into the air. Dust devils whirled across the land, twisting and writhing. The Rangers stopped to cover their horses' muzzles with bandannas. They had already done the same for themselves, pulling their neckerchiefs up over their mouths and noses to filter out some of the dust.

Dakota, who had been promoted to corporal and appointed second-in-command, pulled down his bandanna to speak. He had to shout to be heard over the rising wind.

"Jeb, we can't stay out here," he said. "Not with this storm comin' on."

"I know that," Jeb answered. "But where in the blue blazes do you think we can find someplace to hole up? The wind's comin' straight out of the canyons. We can't make the horses go into it, at least not for long."

"Well, we sure can't turn tail and try to outrun the storm," Tom pointed out. "We'd never make it."

"Jeb," Stan said. "I know where we're at. More important, I know where we can find shelter."

"You do, Stan? Where?" Jeb asked.

"That big canyon off to the northwest. There's an abandoned mining town about a mile in. Unless I miss my guess, most of the buildin's should still be standin'. We can ride out the storm there."

"Are you certain there's a town in that canyon?" Dakota asked. "Far as I know, there ain't nothin' around here but rattlers, buzzards, and scrub brush."

"I'm positive," Stan answered. "I worked that mine, until it played out. Once this storm blows over, there's a trail through the canyon that'll loop around toward the San

Antonio-El Paso road. We'll be able to find our way back to camp from there."

"Then let's head for it, before this storm gets worse," Jeb said. He pulled his bandanna back over his face and led the men toward the canyon. They leaned into the wind as their horses plodded along, heads hung low. Half-an-hour later, they reached the abandoned town. Between the canyon's walls, the wind, while still strong, abated somewhat.

"This is a right cheery place. I'll bet it's just chock-full of haints," Hoot said, looking around at the tumble-down buildings which once had marked a thriving community. There were a few houses, most roofless and windowless, and a two-story hotel. Over its front door, a sign hanging from its one remaining hinge twisted and banged in the wind. Alongside that was the saloon, a faded sign over its entrance proclaiming it as the "Black Gold".

There were what had evidently been several stores, most of which leaned crazily, appearing ready to fall in on themselves at any time. Just outside town, the mine's maw loomed large and black. Its tipple had fallen onto its side. Piles of tailings surrounded it.

"Never mind that," Jeb said. "There's the livery stable, on the far end of town. It looks like it's still in halfway decent shape. Let's get the animals inside before this storm really spooks 'em. Then, I reckon we'll see if the hotel's fit to spend the night in."

"Mebbe we'll be really lucky, and there'll still be a few bottles of red-eye left behind in that saloon," Morey added.

"That's likely," Stan answered. "When the mine flooded, this town closed down real quick. Nobody took the time to pack anything up."

The horses were placed in the livery, unsaddled, and groomed. There was an old pump out back, which still worked, and a couple of buckets hanging on the wall, so they were able to drink their fill. Big Red had recovered from his injury, and Nate was riding him again. He gave the sorrel a pat on the nose, and a piece of biscuit.

Once the mounts were settled, the men took their bedrolls and rifles, some jerky and hardtack from their saddlebags, and headed for the hotel.

"There's just gotta be haints in here," Hoot again said, once they were inside. The lobby's furnishings were still there, most of the upholstery and stuffing gone, chewed away by rodents. Dust covered everything thickly. Cobwebs were draped over the pigeonholes behind the front desk, and the keys still hanging from their pegs. A moth-eaten, faded rug remained on the floor, thick with dirt.

"Hoot, I'm tired of hearin' about your haints," Nate said. "There ain't any haints, or ghosts, or whatever you wanna call 'em."

"There are so," Hoot retorted. "I hear one moanin' now."

"That's just the wind," Nate said.

"Nate's right, Hoot. And it don't matter none," Jeb said. He pulled off his Stetson and slapped it against his leg, to knock off some of the dust. "This storm's kickin' up worse. By dusk, you won't be able to see three feet in front of you, unless this wind dies off. We don't have any choice but to stay right here and ride it out."

"Except to go over to the saloon and see if there's any bottles left," Morey said. "We need somethin' to wash down this jerky and hardtack. That might as well be somethin' to bring a man some pleasure, too."

"If we're gonna do that, we'll have to do it now, before the wind's so strong a man won't be able to stay upright out there," Dakota said.

"That's so," Jeb said. "So let's git."

****

The atmosphere inside the saloon was even more eerie than in the hotel. The back-bar mirror was cracked and dust-streaked. A painting of a well-endowed, scantily clad woman hanging over the mirror had one of its eyes shot out, probably by some drunken miner. The remaining eye seemed to stare at each one of the Rangers. The piano was tipped onto its back. There were three card tables, with cards still scattered across their surfaces. The coal-oil lamps which had hung from the ceiling were now mostly lying crashed and broken on the floor. Cobwebs hung thickly, everywhere. Jeb brushed some off a lamp standing on the bar, its bowl still half-full.

"We'll have light, at least," he said, as he took out a match, struck it to light on his belt buckle, then touched it to the wick. The flame flickered in the drafty room. It revealed several full bottles of whiskey still standing on the back-bar shelf.

"More haints," Hoot hissed. "I can feel 'em, all around us."

"As long as they don't mind sharin' the whiskey, I ain't afraid of a few spooks," Morey said. "Dunno about the rest of you, but I've got a powerful thirst." He went around the back of the bar, took down the bottles, and placed them on the mahogany. He pulled the cork from one, raised it to his lips, and took a long swallow.

"This here stuff ain't the best I've ever tasted, but it's not half-bad," he said, then took another drink. "C'mon, men, join me. I hate to drink alone."

The rest of the bottles were opened and passed around. When one reached Nate, he looked at it dubiously.

"Go on, Nate. Take a swig," Morey urged. "It ain't gonna bite you."

"Nate and Hoot had a bit of a rough go the first time they sampled hard liquor," Carl said. "If either of 'em don't want to take a drink, that's up to them."

"Nah, I'm gonna try this," Nate said. He took a swallow. "Don't seem to have the same kick as tequila."

"Don't let it fool you," Jeb said. "Best you just go easy on that stuff."

"I reckon that's good advice," Nate agreed, then passed the bottle to Hoot.

The Rangers spent the next hour working on jerky and hardtack, washed down with whiskey. Nate had brought along his sketch pad and pencils. He drew several pictures of the saloon, then, while the others kept drinking and smoking, went out on the sidewalk to sketch some of the buildings.

"Stan, how'd you know about this place?" Jeb asked.

"I'm a minin' engineer, originally from Pittston, Pennsylvania," Stan answered. "My specialty is coal minin'. The whole area around Pittston is anthracite country. The ground's just loaded with rich veins of high quality coal, which go on for miles. I worked for the Blue Coal Company up there. A few years back, just after the war was over, they decided to start explorin' the Southwest for coal. So I was sent out here. I found some decent deposits of bituminous and lignite, across the border, down around Piedras Negras, that means "black stones," but what I was really lookin' for was anthracite, which is the hardest, and hottest burnin', coal. I got word there might be some up this way.

"I did find a vein, right here in this canyon, one which held a lotta promise. It wasn't anthracite, but real high quality bituminous. We started minin'. The mine did real well for a couple of years, then the vein began to play out. We drilled deeper, tryin' to find it again. We must've cut into an underground stream when we broke through one wall, because water came pourin' outta there like Noah's flood. Thirteen men drowned, and we're lucky it wasn't more. So the mine, and the town, were abandoned."

"And now the ghosts of those drowned miners are hauntin' this town," Hoot said. "Thirteen of 'em. Unlucky in more ways than one. Jeb, do we really have to stay here?"

"Take a look outside," Jeb answered. "We'll be lucky to make it back to the hotel, between not bein' able to see our noses in front of our faces, and the wind tryin' to blow us away. Sorry, Hoot, we've got no choice but to stay."

Nate had snuck up behind Hoot. He clapped a hand on his shoulder and shouted, "Boo!"

Hoot jumped a foot in the air, whirled around, and hollered bloody murder. "Nate, that weren't funny, ya idjit. You like to scared me half to death."

"I thought it was," Nate said, laughing. "I bet the rest of the boys, did, too."

"Enough of the horseplay," Jeb ordered. "It's high time we got back to the hotel, while we still can."

The wind continued to increase in intensity. Full dark had now fallen, making the short walk back even more difficult. By the time they reached the hotel, the ramshackle building was shaking with each gust. Dust filtered through cracks in the walls and drifted from the ceiling. The wind moaned through the eaves like a woman's screams. Jeb placed the lamp he had brought from the saloon on the desk. He located four more, and also lit those.

"I know it won't be easy, tryin' to sleep, between the dirt, the wind howlin', and the buildin's shakin', but I'd recommend each one of you try'n get some shut-eye. As soon as this storm breaks, we'll be headin' out. Now, who wants to roll out their blankets right here in the lobby, and who might want to see if there's still any beds upstairs?"

"I reckon I'll stay down here," Dakota said. "You ain't gettin' me up there."

"I'll stick with him," Carl answered.

"All right. Morey, Tom?"

"We'll see if there's a room that ain't too filthy," Tom answered. "Any bed in this place probably won't be any worse'n layin' on this floor, and most likely a lot softer than it."

"Okay. Stan, how about you?"

"I'll look for a room," Stan answered.

"Then I'll bunk with you," Jeb said. "That leaves Hoot and Nate. What do you fellers want to do?"

"I'd like to spend the night on a mattress for a change," Nate said. "We've been sleepin' on the hard ground long enough as it is. Hoot?"

"I ain't goin' up there," Hoot said. He eyed the staircase, which was missing half of its banister, and had several of its steps tilting at odd angles, warily. "Not me, no sir."

"C'mon, Hoot," Nate urged. "You don't want to stay down here. Suppose a herd of spooks blows into town. You want to be upstairs, so they might not see you. Down here they'd spot you for certain."

"I dunno," Hoot said, shaking his head.

"Less chance of snakes upstairs," Jeb pointed out. "Other critters, too."

"All right," Hoot said, reluctantly. "But I'm stayin' dressed. Not even takin' my boots or guns off."

"Bullets can't hurt ghosts," Carl said.

"But mebbe they can scare 'em off," Hoot answered. "I might even sleep with my gun in my hand."

"I don't care how you sleep, just as long as your snorin' don't keep me awake," Nate said.

"I probably won't sleep a wink anyway," Hoot said. "Let's go before I change my mind."

The six men who were going to use the bedrooms took three of the lamps, and began to climb the stairs. They stopped when Dakota called after them.

"Hey, fellers, speakin' of spooks, I just remembered what day this is."

"What day might that be, Dakota?" Jeb asked.

"It's October 31st. Halloween."

****

Nate and Hoot chose a room halfway down the hall, between Jeb and Stan's, and Morey and Tom's, rooms. Just like the rest of the hotel, everything was coated with

97

dust, and cobwebs hung thick in the corners. The sole bed sagged in the middle. Tattered curtains fluttered in the wind coming through a hole in the window. Hoot put his lamp on the washstand, then picked up a towel which had been left behind and shoved it in the hole. Some air still came through, but little dust.

"Leastwise, that'll help a bit," he said.

Nate pulled the covers off the bed, threw them in the corner, then pushed on the mattress so it bounced up and down.

"Look, pard. Spooks! They're jumpin' up and down on our bed."

"Real funny, Nate," Hoot said. "If any haints do come after us, I hope they get you first."

They rolled out their blankets on the stained, tattered mattress, then stretched out on their backs, on top of them. Not one article of clothing was removed. Their hats stayed on their heads, their gunbelts around their waists, their boots on their feet. Even their spurs remained on their boots.

"That wind sure does sounds like a woman screamin'," Nate said.

"More like a thousand demons," Hoot answered. "Well, reckon I'll try'n get some sleep. 'Night, Nate."

"'Night, Hoot." Nate tilted his Stetson over his eyes. Despite the tumult of the storm, he drifted off. He had only been sleeping a short while when he was awakened by Hoot's elbow in his ribs.

"Huh? What?" he mumbled.

"Nate! You hear that?" Hoot whispered. "Somethin's clompin' up the stairs. I bet it's a haint. It probably already done ate up Dakota and Carl."

"I thought ghosts didn't make noise," Nate said.

"They can if they want to," Hoot said. "Will you keep your voice down, so it can't hear us?"

From outside, there was the horrible screech of metal

being bent, then torn from its base, The "clomping" stopped as the hotel's sign was ripped off its hinge, and sailed away with the wind.

"There's your haint, Hoot," Nate said. "It was just the doggone sign, bangin' against the wall. Now, let me get back to sleep." He pulled his hat back over his eyes.

"I still say it was a haint," Hoot muttered, as he lay back down.

Twenty minutes later, Hoot was shaking Nate awake again. His eyes were wide with fear.

"Nate, you hear that? There's haints in the walls, scratchin' their way out. They'll be comin' after us any time now."

Nate propped himself up on one elbow. "Hoot, those are just mice, or mebbe rats, in the walls. Probably stirred up by the storm, or by us bein' here. Now, let me sleep!" He shoved Hoot in the chest, pushing him back down, then turned onto his side, with his back to Hoot.

"There are so haints in this town," Hoot grumbled. "Stan said thirteen men died when the mine flooded. Thirteen, an unlucky number. Their spirits are still wanderin' around here, no doubt. And it's Halloween. This is a ghost town we're in, and ghost towns are haunted. That's why they're ghost towns, 'cause they've got ghosts. And they're gonna get us."

An hour later, Nate was awakened yet again by Hoot shaking him.

"Nate, you hear those? Ghost riders!" The sound of horses trotting down the street came clearly through the window and thin walls. Nate sat bolt upright.

"Those are riders, all right, but they ain't no ghosts," he exclaimed. "We'd better find out who they are." He jumped out of the bed, with Hoot on his heels. They grabbed their Winchesters and ran into the hallway. Jeb and Stan were already in the hall. Tom and Morey were standing in their door. All of them had their rifles at the ready.

"Who do you reckon that is, Jeb?" Nate asked.

"I dunno. Either they're travelers caught in this storm, like we are, or they're out here on a night like this for no good reason. But we're sure gonna find out."

Dakota and Carl had also heard the riders, and were waiting when their partners came downstairs.

"Either of you get a glimpse of those hombres?" Jeb asked.

"It was kinda hard, with all the dust flyin' out there, but I'm pretty certain I recognized two of 'em," Dakota answered. "Carlos Zapata and Roy White."

"The men who lead one of the biggest gangs of horse thieves anywhere in Texas, and Mexico," Jeb exclaimed. "They steal horses on both sides of the border, and run 'em across to sell on the other sides. How many men were with 'em, you figure?"

"I counted about twelve riders, all told," Dakota said.

"I got the same," Carl added. "Looks like they're headed for the livery stable. Figures they'd want to put up their mounts."

"Which means they'll find ours, and realize they're not alone here," Jeb said. "We've gotta try'n get the jump on 'em."

"Those boys ain't gonna surrender, at least not without one heckuva fight," Dakota said. "They're all wanted for hangin' offenses. I doubt any one of 'em'll let himself be taken alive."

"Men, we're goin' after that bunch," Jeb said. "Carl, me, you, and Morey'll take the left side of the street. "Dakota, you, Tom, and Nate'll take the right. Hoot, you and Stan duck down the back alley, and try'n circle behind the stable. We don't want those hombres runnin' off our horses, and leavin' us afoot, out here in the middle of nowhere."

"Not to mention, that'd be plumb hard to explain when we got back to camp," Tom said. "In fact, it would be downright embarrassin'.".

"We ain't gonna let that happen," Jeb said. "Mebbe we can catch those boys in a crossfire. But be careful. Make certain of your target before you shoot. We don't want to be pluggin' any of our own pards. Now, let's move."

Shouts and curses from the direction of the livery indicated the horse thieves had discovered the Rangers' mounts.

"They've found our broncs," Dakota said. "Whatever else happens, we can't let 'em get away with our mounts. And if they hole up in the stable, we'll have one devil of a time blastin' 'em outta there without killin' some of the horses. Let's get 'em."

Hoot and Stan were out the door first, followed by Dakota, Tom, and Nate, who, running low, hurried across the street. Jeb, Carl, and Morey were right behind them, staying close to the buildings' walls as they made their way toward the livery.

The horse thieves, fortunately for the Rangers, had dismounted to lead their horses into the stable. Most of them were still outside. Evidently, they had decided to try and find, then rob and kill, whoever owned the horses in the livery, because instead of just running off the horses, they were heading for the center of town. Jeb placed two shots over their heads.

"Texas Rangers!" he shouted. "Zapata, White, and the rest of you, hold it right there. Throw down your guns and get your hands in the air. You're under arrest."

The outlaws responded with bullets and curses, as they dove for cover. Three of them never made it. They were cut down by Ranger lead before they could reach shelter.

The entire street became a maelstrom of bullets, as the lawmen and outlaws blazed away at each other. The swirling dust got into men's eyes, making it difficult to aim. It hid men behind its veil of brown, turning them into shadowy figures, running and ducking in the night. The only chance a man had to strike his target was to aim at a powder flash, and hope to make a hit.

Nate, as did the rest of the Rangers, kept advancing toward the outlaws, hugging the sides of buildings, ducking under hitch rails, diving to his belly and rolling behind horse troughs. Bullets were seeking him out. One hit the wall just next to him, and drove splinters into his cheek. He shot back at the flash of powder from the gunman's pistol, and was rewarded with a yelp of pain, then the thud of a body hitting the dirt. He raced for the corner of the next house, firing as he ran. All around him, gunfire echoed. More shots sounded now, coming from behind the stable. Evidently, Hoot and Stan had made the back of the barn, and were now shooting at the outlaws from behind.

Nate had paused to reload his rifle. He glanced across the street, and saw two of his partners lying flat, firing at three figures in the middle of the road. Their bullets tore into the men, spinning them off their feet.

In less than ten minutes, the battle was over. Silence, which seemed more deafening than the gunfire, descended.

"Boys, is everyone all right?" Jeb shouted. "Don't show yourselves plain, just yet, in case any of those hombres are playin' possum."

"We're okay back here," Hoot called.

One by one, the men answered Jeb, each saying he was unhurt.

"Let's check these renegades," Jeb ordered. "Careful, though."

His caution proved unnecessary. Twelve horse thieves, robbers, and killers lay sprawled dead on the street of that ghost town. The only wounds the Rangers had suffered were the scratches on Nate's cheek, and a bullet burn across Dakota's neck.

"Appears like we just made some new ghosts for this here town," Tom said.

"Seems so," Dakota agreed.

"More haints." Hoot signed in despair. "We've gotta get out of here."

****

By the next morning, the storm had abated. The sun rose in a cloudless, deep blue sky. The outlaws' bodies were dragged to the mine and dropped down a shaft. Their horses would be taken back to the Ranger camp, to be added to the remuda, or returned to their rightful owners, if they could be located.

"Boys, it's gonna be a fine day," Jeb said, as the Rangers mounted up. "Stan's gonna show us the way outta here, and in a few days, we'll be back in camp. That won't be none too soon, either. We're already three days overdue."

He touched his spurs to Dudley's sides, putting the paint into a walk, with the other men strung out behind. Half-a-mile later, they put their horses into a lope, heading back to what was, for the foreseeable future, home.

5

October turned into November, which quickly passed. Unlike at Nate's former home in Delaware, where autumn was marked by the colorful changing of the leaves and sharply colder temperatures, the only indications winter was fast approaching were the gradually shortening days, and a slow cooling of the daytime high temperatures.

Nate did notice two things about the transition from summer, to fall, to winter, in Texas. At this Southern latitude, closer to the equator, the days didn't shorten and nights lengthen quite as much as they did up North. And unlike back home, where by November the cold had killed most vegetation and stripped the trees of their foliage, leaving the landscape drab and brown, here in Texas the cooler weather and slightly increased rainfall actually greened up some of the desert plants.

Captain Quincy had kept all the men in camp for the past week. It was now the last Thursday of November. President Ulysses S. Grant, following a tradition started by President Abraham Lincoln, had declared the day to be a National Day of Thanksgiving. To celebrate, Quincy decided to organize a shooting contest.

"Boys," he said. "This can't be a real turkey shoot, since of course there ain't any turkeys in these parts, like back in east Texas. So, we'll just have to make it a target shoot. We'll have two contests, one for pistol, the other for rifle. And no, Carl, before you ask, you can't enter the long gun contest with your shotgun."

"Aw, Cap'n, that just ain't fair," Carl said, with a grin.

"Guess I'll just have to outshoot you boys with my Winchester."

"That'll never happen," Phil retorted. "I aim to win this contest."

"You pretty much *have* to aim to win a shootin' contest, Phil," Nate pointed out.

"I reckon that's so," Phil agreed. "Although I can generally hit whatever I'm tryin' for without much trouble."

"If y'all'd quit yammerin' we can get started," Quincy said. "Plus, I'd imagine you'd like to hear what the prizes are."

"I know I would," Percy said.

"Whoever wins will receive a bottle from my stock of blended Kentucky bourbon," Quincy said. "I have is shipped down special from home. I guarantee it's the best sippin' whiskey you'll ever taste. There's four bottles left in my supplies, so I'm givin' up half of my remaining stock. Let's get started."

The targets, twigs wedged into holes in a log, had been set up just down canyon from the camp. Of course, no shooting contest would be complete without wagering, so there would also be much betting among the men as to the outcome. The contest for pistols was first. Since being a good shot was a requirement for any Ranger, it took several rounds before some of the men were eliminated. Nate made it to the eighth round, when he missed two shots, and was out. Hoot made it to the tenth, where one missed shot took him out of the competition. Now, six rounds later, the last two contestants were Joe Duffy and Jeb Rollins.

"Last chance to make your bets, boys," Quincy announced. Money changed hands, then Joe stepped to the firing line. He squeezed off six quick shots, and six twigs were splintered. Jeb stepped to the line, and repeated Joe's feat.

"We go again," Quincy said, once the targets were replaced. "Jeb, this time, you go first."

Jeb took his place, and emptied his six-gun. Five twigs disappeared, while one remained standing.

"Looks like I've got ya, Jeb," Joe said. "I can taste that whiskey already." He took his position, and fired, six times. Once he was finished, two twigs stood, untouched.

"Jeb's the winner," Quincy announced. "Nice shootin', both of you."

"Good contest," Joe said, as he and Jeb shook hands. "I'll get you next time."

"I wouldn't be surprised. I'll save a touch of my whiskey for you," Jeb answered. The men who had bet on him were cheering, those who had placed their money on Joe moaning their losses.

"Time for the rifle contest," Quincy called. Once again, targets were set, and the order of shooting drawn.

Nate still hadn't gotten the hang of firing a rifle quite as well as using a pistol. He was the second man eliminated, only George, the cook, missing more shots on his first attempt.

Hoot patted Nate on the shoulder as he dejectedly walked away from the firing line, his head low.

"Don't worry, pard," he said. "You still shoot a Winchester better'n most. Some more practice with your rifle and you'll keep gettin' better."

"Thanks, Hoot," Nate answered. "Let's see who does win this contest. I sure hope it's you."

"That's wishful thinkin'," Hoot answered. "I'm dang good with a rifle, but most of the men are a lot better'n me."

"I'll be rootin' for you anyway," Nate said. "Mebbe even place some money on you."

"Gee, thanks," Hoot said. "I appreciate that. But I wouldn't bet on me, ya idjit. You shouldn't, either."

Much to almost everyone's surprise, except Nate's, Hoot

did make it to the final round. The contest was now down to him and Phil Knight. Knowing Phil's skill with any sort of long gun, almost all the bets were placed on him. Only Nate had wagered on Hoot.

This time, twenty twigs were set up, ten for each man. They were placed a hundred feet farther from the firing line than the previous rounds. Phil went first, and hit seven of ten twigs.

Hoot took in a deep breath, then let it out slowly as he stepped to the line. Sweat beaded on his brow. *Phil had left him an opening. Could he take advantage of it?* He lifted his rifle to his shoulder, sighted down its barrel, and squeezed the trigger. The first twig splintered. He fired again, and missed. Slowly, deliberately, Hoot took aim and fired again. Another twig was cut in two. Hoot fired at the next, then the next. When he was finished, eight of ten twigs were gone. Nate rushed over to him, and grabbed him in a bear hug.

"I told ya you could do it, Hoot!" he shouted. "Didn't I? Didn't I?"

"Yeah, I reckon you did," Hoot said. He had a grin a mile wide across his face. "I don't suppose you bet on me, did you? I warned you not to."

"I sure did," Nate said. "You just won me a whole pile of money."

"You're dang lucky, ya idjit," Hoot said, with a laugh.

Phil came over to congratulate Hoot. "Nice job," he said. "Fine shootin'."

"Thanks, Phil. Better luck next time," Hoot said.

Captain Quincy called Hoot and Jeb over, and gave them their bottles. Dan Morton handed over the winnings for those who had bet on Jeb and Hoot. Nate had been the only one to wager on Hoot. Dan counted a large pile of bills into his outstretched hand.

"I've got to learn to start bettin' with you, not against

you, Nate," he said. "Lost money on the swimmin' race bettin' against you, and now you bet on your buddy, here, and rake in a bundle." He walked away, shaking his head.

"Men, the meat'll be ready right soon now," George called. Percy had shot a mule deer, which had been gutted, and was spitted over a large fire. "If y'all will help get the dishes out of the wagon, you'll eat quicker."

The hungry Rangers needed no urging to jump to that chore. Once they had their plates and utensils, Captain Quincy had the men set them aside, and gather around him.

"Men, please remove your hats," he said. Once that was done, he continued. "I'd like us all to take a moment to offer thanks. We have many things to be thankful for. We've lost no members of our company since our arrival here in the Big Bend, despite our having crossed paths with many bands of outlaws. We're away from our families, those of us who have them, but I consider all of you family—Ranger family. We have food, drink, and shelter. So, let us thank God, each in his own way, silently."

The men bowed their heads, each giving thanks, according to his beliefs.

"Thank you," Quincy said, a few minutes later. "I also want to take a moment to remember the fine Rangers we have lost over the past months: Tim Tomlinson, Tom's twin brother; Andy Pratt, Tad Cooper, Tex Carlson, Ed Jennings, Bill Tuttle, Shorty Beach, Hank Glynn, and Lee Shelton. Let us take a moment of silence to remember our fallen comrades, each one of them a Ranger, brave and true. Leave us also remember our partner Nate's father, mother, and brother, who were so suddenly, and cruelly, taken from him."

Once again, the assembled men bowed their heads, silently remembering their friends, who had died bringing justice to Texas, as well as Nate's family.

"Thanks, men. Now, let's eat!"

The men lined up at the chuck wagon. Shortly, they were all seated cross-legged around the fire, chewing on venison. George had made a trip into Presidio for supplies, so the meat was accompanied by potatoes roasted over the hot coals, pinto beans, and butternut squash. Dessert would be dried-apple pies, baked in George's Dutch oven.

"Boy howdy, I'm more stuffed than the turkey my ma used to roast for Thanksgiving," Nate said, as he leaned back against a tree and patted his belly. "George, you are one fine cook."

"Thank you, son," George said, then, more loudly, "See here, you galoots, it's only the youngster who appreciates my cookin'. So he gets the last piece of pie. Rest of you don't bother to ask me for any extra."

"We all enjoy your cookin', George," Lieutenant Bob said. "We're just too full to even move right now, let alone tell you how good it is."

The Rangers sat around the fire until night fell. Joe Duffy pulled out his harmonica and began playing. He started with "Buffalo Gals", followed by "Pop Goes the Weasel", then the old hymns "Farther Along" and "Wayfaring Stranger". One by one, the men headed for their tents.

"Nate, before we turn in, why don't we polish off this here bottle of whiskey I won?" Hoot suggested.

"You mean get downright drunk, like back in San Saba?" Nate said.

"Sure. Why not? We don't have to ride out tomorrow, and we're not in town. We can't cause any harm or get into trouble, way out here."

"Why not?" Nate said.

The two youngsters walked upstream for a short distance, then sat down, with their backs against a large boulder. Hoot pulled the bottle of bourbon from his back pocket, uncorked it, and took a swallow. It burned his throat a bit, but went down easily.

"Boy howdy, Cap'n Dave wasn't kiddin'," he said, as he passed the bottle to Nate. "This stuff goes down real smooth, and warms my belly just fine."

Nate rubbed his sleeve over the bottle top, then took a drink. As Hoot said, the bourbon was nowhere near as harsh as tequila, nor the corn liquor they had appropriated from the buffalo hunters.

"You're right, Hoot. This is good stuff." He took another drink, then handed the bottle back.

In forty-five minutes, they had polished off the bottle's contents. Hoot attempted to stand up, but fell flat on his face.

"I think...I think...you've had enough, pardner," Nate said, slurring his words.

"Oh, yeah? I'll have you know I can hold my liquor, Nate, ya idjit," Hoot retorted. He rolled onto his back.

"So can I. Lemme show you," Nate said. He also attempted to stand, but sagged back against the rock. "Well, maybe later. But Hoot, why do you keep callin' me an idiot?"

"Because it kinda fits, and I like ya," Hoot said. "It's just sorta a nickname for ya, from when ya first joined up, and didn't have any idea what Rangerin' was all about. I don't mean no harm by it."

"Long as you say so," Nate said.

"I'm gonna try and get up," Hoot said. He managed to roll over, get on his hands and knees, crawled back to the rock, and sat next to Nate.

"We're gonna be pards forever, ain't we, Nate?"

"We sure are, Hoot. Pards forever, through thick and thin."

"Pards forever. Nate..." Hoot stopped, for whatever he was about to say, Nate wouldn't hear. He had passed out, and was leaning against Hoot, his head on Hoot's shoulder.

"Reckon that's not a bad idea," Hoot muttered. "Think I'll..." His head fell limply against Nate's, as he also passed out.

Twenty minutes later, Jeb, who had been sent after them, came upon them. Both were snoring loudly. Jeb took the empty bottle from Hoot's hand and shook his head.

"You two are sure gonna have achin' heads and queasy bellies come mornin'," he said. "Well, I reckon I might as well leave you right here until then." He tossed the empty bottle into the creek, then headed back to camp.

6

Another month passed. It was now only a few days until Christmas. While the daytime temperatures still often reached into the fifties and sixties, at night they plummeted well below freezing. Nate had ridden into Presidio along with some of the other men, where he purchased a heavy sheepskin coat. That coat had served him well during a recent cold snap. For the past two days, though, the air had warmed considerably. This afternoon, the temperature had climbed well into the seventies. Nate and Hoot were grooming Big Red and Dusty.

"Nate," Hoot asked. "If you could have anythin' you wanted for Christmas, what would it be?"

"I'd like to have my folks back with me," Nate answered. "Since that's not possible, there's nothin' else I really want. Well, mebbe a new saddle blanket for Red, but that's about it. How about you?"

"I'd really like to get to finally kiss a gal," Hoot said. "I might buy one a ribbon for her hair. Mebbe that'd get her to kiss and hug on me. Wouldn't you like a gal, too?"

"I reckon," Nate said. "But as long as we're stuck way out here, we ain't ever gonna find one. Mebbe if we ever get back to Austin."

"Well, someday we'll both have us gals. You can bet your hat on it," Hoot said. He tossed down Dusty's currycomb, and picked up his dandy brush. He ran the soft brush over his horse's thick winter coat, then put that down, and took out his hoof pick. When he bent over to lift Dusty's near front hoof, Nate kicked him in the rump, sending him sprawling.

"Nate! What'd you go and do that for?" Hoot exclaimed, indignantly.

"I just couldn't help myself, seein' your butt stickin' out like that," Nate said.

"Well, it wasn't very smart, ya idjit," Hoot answered. He picked himself up and dusted himself off. "Suppose I'd fallen under my horse. I could've gotten hurt, real bad."

"You're right," Nate conceded. "I'm sorry. I wasn't thinkin', and I won't do it again."

"It's okay," Hoot said. "Just do me one more favor, and try'n keep your big feet outta my way. I get tired of trippin' over your boots when I get outta bed. Those things are big enough to fit an elephant."

Nate turned red. "I'm sick and tired about everyone sayin' how big my feet are." With that, he launched a vicious punch to the middle of Hoot's belly. Hoot folded into another blow, to his chin. That one knocked him on his back. His head struck a rock. Hoot moaned once, then lay unmoving. Blood trickled from one ear, and from his mouth.

"Hoot!" Nate shouted. "Hoot!" He knelt beside his friend, shaking his shoulder. "Hoot!" There was no response.

"Jim!" Nate shouted. "Jim! Hoot's hurt, bad. Come quick!"

Jim was in front of the tent he shared with Hoot, Nate, and Dan, reading Shakespeare's *King Lear.* Hearing Nate's frantic shouts, he tossed aside the book and hurried to him. Jeb, Captain Quincy, Lieutenant Berkeley, and Ken Demarest were right behind him.

"Nate! What happened?" Jim asked.

"I dunno. I mean, I hit Hoot. He was kiddin' me about my big feet again. That made me mad, so I hit him. But I didn't hit him that hard, at least, I didn't think I had. Now, I can't get him to wake up."

Jim skinned open one of Hoot's eyelids. The eye's pupil was dilated, and unresponsive. Jim shook his head.

"Jim! How bad is it?" Nate cried.

"I'm not certain yet. Hoot might've cracked his skull on that rock, or he might have a bad concussion. No matter what it is, it's not good. A couple of you help me carry him to our tent, so I can take a better look at him."

"You mean I might've killed him?" Nate exclaimed.

"I dunno," Jim said. "I just don't know. Let's get him moved."

Jeb took Hoot by his shoulders, Ken by his ankles. They picked him up, and carried him to the tent. Nate followed along. Jim stopped him when he tried to duck inside.

"You'd better stay outside, Nate. You've done enough damage already."

Several of the other men had seen Hoot being carried to the tent. They shouted questions at Nate.

"What the blazes happened to Hoot?" Larry asked.

"It's all my fault," Nate said, sobbing. "I slugged him for complainin' about my big feet again. He didn't mean nothin' by it, but he made me mad, so I slugged him. He hit his head on a rock, and busted it open. I killed my best friend."

"Hoot's...dead?" Joe echoed.

"Well, mebbe not yet, but he's dyin'. I just know he is," Nate said.

"Nate, listen to me. You don't know that for certain, at least not yet," Joe told him. "And you didn't mean to hurt him. It was an accident. You know we get into scrapes all the time, while we're stuck in camp. We fight, then it's over, and we're friends again. It was just bad luck Hoot's head hit that rock. It was an accident."

"No, it wasn't," Nate insisted. "I hit him more'n once. I could've just slugged him in the gut, but no. I had to hit him again."

"Nate, what's done is done," Tom said. "Frettin' about what happened won't change it. You need to calm down, and get a-holt of yourself. Tell you what? Why don't you and I take a walk, just get away from here for a couple of minutes. You'll see things more clearly, once you're thinkin' straight."

"That's good advice," Joe said. "Go with Tom, Nate. Please. We'll let you know about Hoot, soon as we find out somethin'."

"C'mon," Tom took him by the arm and led him away from the tent, where Jim was examining Hoot.

Tom took Nate about two hundred feet downstream, toward the Rio. They stopped at a point where Blue Creek had dug its channel a bit deeper, and climbed to the top of some rocks which overlooked the creek, fifty feet below.

"Dunno about you, Nate, but watchin' a stream always makes me feel better," Tom said. "Helps me to relax, and sort things out in my mind. Let's just stay here a spell. Talk to me if you want, scream and yell if you feel the need, cry if you have to. But don't keep what happened bottled up inside. It'll eat you up if you do."

"But I killed him," Nate insisted.

"You still don't know that," Tom answered. "And yes, you did mean to hit Hoot. There's no denyin' that. But you can't take back that punch. And you didn't mean to hurt him. Keep tellin' yourself that. And that Hoot's gonna be all right."

"I dunno." Nate bent down and picked up a handful of pebbles. He began tossing them into the stream, one at a time. "Mebbe I wasn't meant to be a Ranger. Mebbe I should quit, right now."

"Don't even talk like that," Tom snapped. "You're a fine Ranger, a man each and every one of us is proud to ride with. Not the scared boy you were when we found you, but a man. You're no quitter. You're a fighter. You've proved that already, more'n once. No one blames you for what happened. You lost your temper, just like all of us do at one time or another. That's no reason to quit the outfit, or give up on yourself."

"I dunno," Nate repeated. He took a step closer to the edge of the rock. His right foot landed on a patch of moss, growing where the rock sloped toward the creek. His foot shot out from under him. With a scream, Nate toppled over the edge and fell into the water, with a splash.

"Nate!" Tom yelled. "Nate!"

There had been rain for several days in the mountains where Blue Creek had its source, so the stream was running high and fast. Nate disappeared under the water. He surfaced once, then the current pulled him around a bend, out of Tom's sight. It took all the strength Tom had to keep from diving in after him. He started back to camp on the run. Jeb met him on the way.

"Tom. We heard Nate yell. What happened to him?"

"He slipped, and fell in the creek," Tom said. "I'm goin' for my horse to try'n find him."

"Get Percy to go with you. If anyone can find Nate, he can."

"Right." Tom found the Tonkawa scout and told him what had happened. A few minutes later, they were galloping their horses out of camp.

Percy and Tom spent over an hour combing the creek banks. Finally, Percy shook his head.

"It's no use, Tom. That water's runnin' too fast, and too high. The current most likely sucked Nate under. His body's probably in the Rio Grande by now. He's gone."

"I know," Tom answered. "I hate givin' up, but I know. Reckon we might as well go back and break the news."

7

Nate awakened, face down on a sand bar. He had no recollection of how he got there. The last thing he remembered was falling into Blue Creek, then being carried away by its rushing waters. He didn't recall bring pulled under, then his body being tossed over some rapids. He didn't recall his struggle to swim to shore, his efforts thwarted by the current, and his boots and clothes dragging him down. He didn't recall the turbulent current carrying him into the Rio Grande, then taking him into shallow water, where he was able to crawl out of the river, get to his feet, and stumble for a few yards before he collapsed, exhausted by his struggles. He had no idea how long he had lain there, nor how far he had been carried downstream. Chilled to the bone, he shivered, violently. He rolled onto his back, then sat up. The sun was only about a half-hour from setting.

"First thing I've gotta do is get outta these wet duds," he muttered. "Then, I've got to try and get a fire goin'."

He pulled off his boots and socks, then stripped off his clothes, and spread them out on the sand. He stood up, looking around for any source of fuel. There were some dried reeds along the riverbank, as well as some pieces of driftwood, left behind when the water receded after some past flood. Nate ripped down most of the reeds, piled them on the sand, then placed several small pieces of wood atop them. He picked up two sharp rocks, and knelt alongside the kindling.

"Here's hopin' I can remember what Jeb taught me

about how to start a fire, and that these here rocks are the right ones."

Nate began striking the rocks against each other, hoping desperately for a spark. It took him better than twenty tries, but finally a spark hit the reeds, and a tiny flame appeared. Nate blew gently on it, urging it to life. The dry reeds quickly took hold, then the kindling wood. Nate added some logs to the blaze, and placed more near it. With the fire going, he spread out his clothes alongside it to dry. He hunkered in front of it.

"Good thing we're havin' a warm spell," he said. "It won't get all that cold tonight." He looked around at his surroundings, and realized, with a start, where he was.

"Son of a gun, I'm in Mexico," he exclaimed. "The current must've carried me across. Well, there's nothin' to do about it tonight. The sun's about gone. I'll spend the night here, get some rest, then try'n cross back to Texas come mornin'."

He tossed more wood on the fire, stretched out on his back, and was soon sleeping.

****

The next morning, Nate was awakened by the rays of the sun, which was already high in the sky, warming his flesh. He sat up with a jerk.

"I slept longer'n I meant to," he muttered. "I've got to get movin'. The men must think I drowned. They won't even be lookin' for me. I've got to try'n get back, to find out what happened to Hoot. Dunno what I'm gonna do once I get back, but I can't just run out on the Rangers. Not after all they've done for me."

The fire had died out, but Nate's clothes were now dry. At least they were at the moment, but they wouldn't be for long. They'd be soaked again, once he swam back across the river. He decided it wasn't worth the effort to redress, but rolled the clothes in a bundle, tying them with his shirtsleeves. He tucked the clothes under his left arm, picked up his boots with his right hand, and began walking upriver, looking for any sign of a ford, or crossing. Several times he hurt his bare feet on sharp stones, but walking over the rough, rock-strewn riverbank in his heavy, still-damp boots would be even worse, and would soon lead to raw, blistered feet.

He'd gone about a mile when he came upon a spot where the Rio ran shallower. Ripples on its surface indicated Nate might be able to walk across to Texas—at least, most of the way.

"Well, here goes." Nate stepped into the water. It rose more quickly than he expected, soon up to his knees, then his belly. He held his clothes and boots over his head as it reached his chest. Any deeper, and he would be forced to swim.

Without warning, Nate stepped into a hidden hole, a soft spot where the Rio's swirling currents had dug out sand and mud. He plunged in over his head, and lost his grip on his clothes and boots. He surfaced, spluttering, watching helplessly as the current carried his clothes away. And there was no chance of finding his boots, somewhere under the muddy water. Nate cursed, and struck out for the Texas shore. He had to swim most of the way, for the Rio had dug its main channel close to the Texas riverbank at this point. Nate cursed again when he emerged from the river.

"This is just great! I've got no food, no clothes, no gun, not that I'd know where to put a gun if I did have one, and have no idea where I'm at, except somewhere in Texas. Only thing I can do is start walkin', and hope the sun doesn't broil me to death."

Nate began following the Rio's twisting course, hoping he hadn't been carried too far from Blue Creek, and the

Ranger camp, by its swift moving waters. The unusually hot—for this time of year—weather, which until now had been his friend became his mortal enemy. The blistering sun soon had his skin burned red and raw. Thorny brush clawed at his flesh, spiny cactus tore at him. Sharp rocks cut and bruised his feet. Still, determined to get back to camp, Nate pressed on. By the time night fell, he was stumbling, limping badly on the right ankle he had twisted, barely able to keep moving. Too worn out to go any farther, he found a nest of boulders, still emanating warmth from the day's sun, and curled up in them.

****

Nate was startled out of his sleep by a sharp voice.

"Get outta there, you sneakin' Apache," it ordered. Nate opened his eyes to see a lanky young cowboy, probably a couple of years younger than himself, atop a long-legged chestnut gelding. The cowboy held a six-gun pointed directly at his stomach.

"Huh?" Nate said.

"You heard me. C'mon on outta those rocks. And keep your hands where I can see 'em. Don't try anythin', or I'll gut shoot you right where you're at, and let the buzzards pick at your bones. I wouldn't mind pluggin' you at all, no sir, not at all, Indian."

"I'm no Indian," Nate protested. He started to push himself up.

"No fast moves. Slow and easy," the cowboy ordered. "You Apaches are real quick."

"I told you, I'm no Indian. Not Apache, or Comanche, or Kiowa, or what have you," Nate repeated. He stood up, careful not to make any sudden moves, and keeping his hands in plain sight. He was certain the young cowboy meant exactly what he said. One wrong move, and he'd put a chunk of lead through Nate's guts.

"Well, you sure look like one," the cowboy insisted. "You're red like an Indian, and you're runnin' around all buck-naked like an Indian, except they mostly at least wear a breechclout. I reckon you must've lost yours when I chanced upon you runnin' off some of our horses, and took a shot at you. You sure took off like the heel flies was after you. You're one of the bunch of renegade Apaches who have been sneakin' across the border from Mexico, and raidin' ranches all up and down the river."

"That wasn't me you saw. Take a closer look," Nate said. "I'm white, not Indian. Got a bad sunburn. Plus, you ever seen an Indian wearin' a beard?"

"You ain't got no beard," the cowboy said.

"Do so," Nate answered.

The cowboy took a closer look. "Boy howdy, I guess you do, at least sort of. I wouldn't go around braggin' about it, though, if I was you. You can't hardly see it. Well, if you ain't an Apache, who the heck are you, and how'd you come to be holed up in those rocks?"

"My name's Nate...Nate Stewart. I'm a Texas Ranger. I'm with Captain Dave Quincy's company, camped up along Blue Creek. I fell into the creek, got swept away, and nearly drowned. Somehow, I ended up on the Mexican shore. I had to spend the night there, to get some strength back, before I tried to make it back to camp. Had to shuck my clothes, since they were soaked from my dunkin' in the river, so I could warm up some. I didn't put 'em back on, knowin' I'd have to cross the Rio again. Found what I thought was a decent ford, but I stepped into a deep spot and lost my clothes, and my boots. I made it back across, walked as far as I could, then when it got dark took shelter here for the night. Then you came along, and scared me plumb half to death, wakin' me out of a sound sleep and pointin' that gun at me."

"What kind of sandy are you tryin' to run on me,

mister?" the cowboy asked. "You might not be an Indian, but you sure ain't no Texas Ranger. Heck, you're not much older than me, it appears. You're too young to be a Ranger."

"I got taken on after my folks and brother got killed in a raid on our ranch. I was shot and left for dead. Some Rangers found me, patched me up, and ended up takin' me along with 'em. Look, I don't have time to go into all that. I'm in trouble, and need some help, bad," Nate said. "One of my pards got hurt. I'm not sure what kind of shape he's in. I need to get back to see how he's doin'. You gonna give me any? If not, just let me be on my way."

"You sure ain't gonna make it back to Blue Creek, where you claim the Rangers are camped, on foot," the cowboy answered. "It's over six miles, through some mighty rough country. I reckon the best thing to do is take you back to the ranch I work for. It's the Circle Dot E. The headquarters is about four miles from here. I imagine Charlie Hennessey—he's the boss—can figure out what to do with you. I can't leave you out here, to the mercy of the Apaches and buzzards, that's for dang sure. My handle's Zack, by the way. Zack Ellesio. Hop on up behind me. Shenandoah, here, will carry double, at least until we get to where I left the other horses. You can ride one of them the rest of the way."

"You happen to have any spare duds in your saddlebags I can borrow, Zack?" Nate asked.

"I sure don't," Zack said. "Tell you what. You can cover yourself with this." He untied the blanket from the back of his saddle, and tossed it to Nate.

"Much obliged," Nate said, as he wrapped the blanket around himself. The rough wool was scratchy, made him itch like the devil, and was pure torture on his sunburned skin, but at least it provided protection from him getting even more burned.

"I reckon you can use a drink, and a bite to eat," Zack said. "Here." He passed Nate his canteen, then opened his saddlebag and removed a piece of jerky, which he gave to Nate. "It ain't much, but if you're as starved as I suspect you are, it'll be mighty tasty."

"Thanks," Nate said. He gulped down the tough, stringy, dried meat, then took a long drink from the canteen and handed it back to Zack.

"*Por nada*," Zack said. "Now, scramble on up here so we can get movin'."

Nate did as instructed. Zack heeled his chestnut into a walk. It was only a short distance to the small glade where Zack had left the other horses, which evidently some Apaches had tried to steal. Nate gave a small shudder as he slid off of Shenandoah. If those Apaches had come across him, he'd be dead, and one of them would be now wearing Nate's scalp on his belt. Unconsciously, he reached up to run a hand through his hair.

"You'd better take Lacey," Zack said. "That's the strawberry mare. She's the gentlest in this bunch, and has the smoothest gait. And she'll follow right along. Since I don't have a halter or bridle for her, that's kinda important."

"All right." Nate walked slowly up to the mare, who didn't shy at his approach. Between his burned skin and the unwieldy blanket he wore, it took a bit of doing to climb onto Lacey's bare back. Nate sighed as he settled onto the horse. The trip to the Circle Dot E would be uncomfortable at best, painful at worst, but at least he was no longer lost, and afoot.

"You ready? Then let's go," Zack said. He put his horse into a slow walk, herding the others ahead of him.

"We're gonna have to move slow, Nate, to take it easy on you, so we won't make the ranch until after dark," he said.

"What d'ya mean, Zack? It's only mid-mornin'. We won't

be movin' *that* slow," Nate objected.

"Take a look again," Zack answered. "The sun's goin' down, not climbin'. You must've slept clear through the mornin', and half the afternoon besides."

Nate glanced at the sun. Sure enough, it was late afternoon. Surely his partners had given him up for dead... if they'd even searched for him at all.

****

It was full dark when Nate and Zack finally reached the Circle Dot E. Two rows of lit candles, set in paper sacks, illuminated the trail to its entrance. Every window in the main house blazed with light.

"Sure glad to see the place," Zack said. "I ain't been home for more'n ten days."

"What're all those lights for, Zack?" Nate asked.

"Those? Those are *luminarias*," Zack answered. "The Mexicans light 'em, to help the Holy Family find their way to the inn on Christmas Eve. Miz Louella, that's Mrs. Hennessey, the boss's wife, picked up the tradition. Those lights are sure pretty, ain't they?"

"You mean it's Christmas Eve?" Nate asid.

"It sure is," Zack answered.

Nate fell silent. Not only had he lost his family this past year, but also, apparently, his Ranger partners. He'd be spending Christmas among strangers.

It only took a short while to ride into the ranch yard. The horses were turned into the first corral.

"I'll take care of 'em later, Nate," Zack said, as he tossed Shenandoah's saddle and blanket on the fence. "Right now, it's more important you get yourself patched up. Let's head for the house. All the boys will be there, for the big Christmas Eve spread Miz Louella puts out."

Nate followed Zack to the house, through the front door, and down the hall.

"Charlie. Miz Louella," Zack called. "Brought home a stray hombre. I found him hurt, down along the river."

"Well, bring him on in," a woman's voice answered.

"C'mon, Nate," Zack said. Nate wrapped the blanket more tightly around himself before he walked into the parlor...and stopped dead in his tracks.

"Cap'n Dave! Jeb! And Hoot! All of you!" Every member of Captain Quincy's company was there in that parlor.

"Nate!" Quincy's drink fell from his hand, so surprised was he at seeing the young Ranger he'd thought dead standing there. Nate looked like death warmed over, but he was alive! "What...how...We'd given you up as a goner. Don't you ever give us a scare like that again."

"I'm not really sure how I got out of the water, Cap'n," Nate said. "I woke up on the Mexican side of the river. Lost my clothes tryin' to swim back. Zack, here, found me, and brought me back with him. But what're you fellers doin' here?"

"The Hennesseys invited us for Christmas, after we recovered some of their cattle rustlers had run off," Quincy explained. "In fact, we're gonna make our headquarters here, on their ranch, until our work in this territory is finished. It's centrally located, so it's a good place for us."

"And we have an extra bunkhouse that won't be needed again until spring branding, which means you won't have to sleep in tents, or on the ground," Hennessey added.

"None of that matters," Nate said. "Hoot. You're all right. I thought for certain I'd killed you, pard. I'm sure sorry."

"Heck, it'd take a lot more'n a sock to my gut and hittin' my head on a rock to finish me off, ya idjit," Hoot answered. "As for bein' sorry, there's no need. What happened's already forgotten. Besides, long as we're ridin' together, it won't be our last scrap. We'll be tradin' punches more'n once. You can count on that. I'm just dang glad to see you survived that dunkin'."

"Wait just a doggone minute," Zack said. "You mean this here hombre really *is* a Ranger?"

"He sure is," Captain Quincy replied. "One of the finest Rangers a man can ride the river with."

"Enough talk," Mrs. Hennessey ordered. "You can catch up on all of this later. Right now, this boy needs to have his hurts tended to, get some clothes on his back, get some food in him, and get to bed. Nate, come with me. I have some of my son's clothes that should fit you."

Mrs. Hennessey took Nate into the kitchen. His cuts were washed out, his sunburned skin coated with salve, then he was given a nightshirt to slip over his head. He was allowed a light meal, then hustled off to bed.

****

The next day, Christmas, was a whirlwind of activity. Nate was introduced to the rest of the Hennessey family, the sons, Brian, Josiah, and Luke, and the daughters, Claire and Clarissa. Mr. Hennessey led a brief prayer service, in honor of the Lord's birth. Food and drink were plentiful. Everyone ate their fill. Three of the Circle Dot E cowboys brought out fiddles and bows, another a guitar. The parlor rug was rolled back, so everyone could dance. Nate couldn't help but notice that Hoot and Clarissa Hennessey seemed to spend most of the afternoon together.

Finally, the festivities wound down. Exhausted, Nate wandered outside. He found Hoot out in the yard, sitting on a bench, smoking a cigarette, and gazing at the stars.

"Hoot, I'm glad to finally have the chance to talk with you," Nate said. "Did you really mean what you said last night, that what happened is forgotten?"

"I sure did," Hoot answered. "Like we said awhile back, pardners forever. Except for one thing. Clarissa. She's mine, long as we're in these parts, anyway. So hands off

126

her, or I'll have to plug you...right through your belly, so you'd die slow and painful."

Hoot laughed, to take the sting out of his words.

"Don't worry, Hoot," Nate said. "I'm happy you finally found a gal. Mebbe someday I'll find one, too. Now, I'm gonna say good night to Big Red, then turn in. Good night."

"G'night, Nate."

Nate walked to the corral which held the Rangers' horses. He whistled, and Red trotted up to him.

"Howdy, fella," Nate said. "I snatched a biscuit for you." He gave Red the treat, then rubbed his velvety nose while the horse chewed. "For a while there, I never thought I'd see you again."

Nate stood by the fence, petting his horse, and lost in thought. He turned at the sound of soft footsteps, to see a young Mexican girl approaching.

"*Senor* Nate?" she said. "Would you like some company?"

"I reckon," Nate answered. He could feel the heat rushing to his face. His heart seemed to skip a beat.

"I am Consuela...Consuela Ortiz," the girl said. "You didn't notice me last night, tired as you were, but I helped *Senora* Hennessey care for you. I hope you do not mind."

"Not, not at all," Nate stammered. Actually, the thought of this pretty Mexican girl tending to him was a pleasant one, indeed.

"I understand you are an orphan," Consuela went on. "I, also, am an orphan. My family was killed by *banditos*, at our home in Ojinaga. I needed work, which is how I came to live here, with the Hennesseys. They are very kind to me. But, I was hoping, since you and I have something in common, that we could perhaps be friends. Would you like that? I know you must miss your family horribly, especially at this time of the year. I know I feel terribly lonely at

Christmas, without *mi madre y mi padre, y mis hermanos y hermanas*, to share the joy of the season. I thought perhaps we might help each other through our sorrows."

"I'd like that very much," Nate answered. "I *am* feeling kind of down, even though I have my Ranger pardners as friends. I miss my ma and pa and big brother somethin' fierce. I'd like to have a special friend to talk with."

"Fine. *Gracias, Senor* Nate," Consuela said.

"Whoa," he said with a smile. "Just plain Nate."

"*Si. Gracias*...Nate. Now, I must go. It is not proper for a man and a woman to be alone, together, in the night. We will meet tomorrow, perhaps. *Feliz Navidad*."

She lifted her face, reaching up to kiss Nate on the cheek, then turned and walked away. Nate rubbed his cheek. The spot where her lips had touched burned like fire. He felt a warmth, clear down to his toes.

"Not perhaps...*definitely*," he whispered. He watched the moon as it began its trek across the sky. In just a few days, a new year would begin. A new year, and perhaps, another new beginning.

*P. 78: *When Pecos County was organized, in 1875, Saint Gall became the county seat. In 1881 Saint Gall's name was officially changed to Fort Stockton.*

Look For Lone Star Ranger 5: A Ranger to Stand With. Coming Soon.

About the Author

Jim Griffin became enamored of the Texas Rangers from watching the TV series, Tales of the Texas Rangers, as a youngster. He grew to be an avid student and collector of Rangers' artifacts, memorabilia and other items. His collection is now housed in the Texas Ranger Hall of Fame and Museum in Waco.

His quest for authenticity in his writing has taken him to the famous Old West towns of, Pecos, Deadwood, Cheyenne, Tombstone and numerous others. While Jim's books are fiction, he strives to keep them as accurate as possible within the realm of fiction.

A graduate of Southern Connecticut State University, Jim now divides his time between Branford, Connecticut and Keene, New Hampshire when he isn't travelling around the west.

A devoted and enthusiastic horseman, Jim bought his first horse when he was a junior in college. He has owned several American Paint horses. He is a member of the Connecticut Horse Council Volunteer Horse Patrol, an organization which assists the state park Rangers with patrolling parks and forests.

Jim's books are traditional Westerns in the best sense of the term, portraying strong heroes with good character and moral values. Highly reminiscent of the pulp westerns of yesteryear, the heroes and villains are clearly separated.

Jim was initially inspired to write at the urging of friend and author James Reasoner. After the successful publication of his first book, Trouble Rides the Texas Pacific, published in 2005, Jim was encouraged to continue his writing.

A RANGER TO RIDE WITH by James J. Griffin

Nathaniel Stewart's life changes in the blink of an eye when his family is murdered by a band of marauding raiders. They've made one terrible mistake...they didn't finish the job. Fourteen-year-old Nathaniel is very much alive and ready to exact the justice his mother, father, and older brother deserve. Taken in by a company of Texas Rangers, he begins to learn what it means to survive in the rugged wilds of Texas.

A RANGER TO RECKON WITH by James J. Griffin

As the youngest man in the company of Texas Rangers he's riding with, Nate Stewart discovers he's got a lot to learn. Determined to find the brutal gang of raiders who murdered his family and left him for dead on the Texas plains, Nate must grow up fast. When he comes face-to-face with the pale-eyed devil responsible for the deaths of his parents and older brother, will Nate be able to finally get his revenge?

A RANGER TO FIGHT WITH by James J. Griffin

When Captain Quincy's company of Rangers is ordered to the Big Bend, Nate has no choice but to ride with them. It appears his odds of finding the men who murdered his family grow more distant with each passing mile. Will Nate and his Ranger companions finally catch up with the killers? Nate's gut feeling says they will—but who will survive?

Made in the USA
Middletown, DE
16 August 2015